Eddie's hold around Sherri's neck eased mercifully.

But she still struggled to pull in a full breath as her gaze clung to Cole. His soft gray eyes that had once sparkled with mischievous teasing now brimmed with a tangle of regret and despair.

"I wasn't going to hurt nobody," Eddie muttered.

"I know." That telltale muscle twitch in Cole's cheek gave Sherri an odd pang of reassurance. "But I can't help you if you don't drop the knife."

"You don't wanna help me!" Eddie shoved Sherri into Cole's line of fire and ran toward the rear door.

Thrown off balance, she tumbled right into Cole's arms. They closed protectively around her. And for a few blissful seconds she felt fifteen again.

"Thank you for getting me out in one piece."

He cradled her jaw in his palm. "You were amazing back there."

She stiffened, not wanting to acknowledge how something inside her came alive at his touch, at the admiration in his gaze.

"I'm sorry," he whispered, and she had the uncomfortable feeling he was apologizing for a lot more than his out-of-control brother.

Sandra Orchard hails from beautiful Niagara, Canada, where inspiration abounds for her award-winning novels. She's passionate about writing stories that both keep the reader guessing and reveal God's love and faithfulness through the lives of her characters. She loves to hear from readers and can be reached through her website, sandraorchard.com.

EMERGENCY REUNION

SANDRA ORCHARD

HARLEQUIN® LOVE INSPIRED® SUSPENSE

Recycling programs
for this product may
not exist in your area.

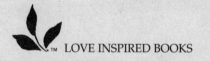 LOVE INSPIRED BOOKS

ISBN-13: 978-0-373-67691-0

Emergency Reunion

Copyright © 2015 by Sandra van den Bogerd

All rights reserved. Except for use in any review, the reproduction or utilization of this work in whole or in part in any form by any electronic, mechanical or other means, now known or hereinafter invented, including xerography, photocopying and recording, or in any information storage or retrieval system, is forbidden without the written permission of the editorial office, Love Inspired Books, 233 Broadway, New York, NY 10279 U.S.A.

This is a work of fiction. Names, characters, places and incidents are either the product of the author's imagination or are used fictitiously, and any resemblance to actual persons, living or dead, business establishments, events or locales is entirely coincidental.

This edition published by arrangement with Love Inspired Books.

® and TM are trademarks of Love Inspired Books, used under license. Trademarks indicated with ® are registered in the United States Patent and Trademark Office, the Canadian Intellectual Property Office and in other countries.

www.Harlequin.com

Printed in U.S.A.

But He said to me, "My grace is sufficient for you, for My power is made perfect in weakness." Therefore I will boast all the more gladly about my weaknesses, so that Christ's power may rest on me.
—2 Corinthians 12:9

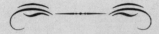

To Charlotte Cripps and Stacey Weeks. Thank you!

ONE

At the sight of her ambulance's side door yawning open, Sherri Steele tripped to a stop. This afternoon was headed the same way as the unsettled June weather. Stormy. Again.

"What's the holdup?" her partner groused from the other end of the stretcher straddling their patient's threshold.

She motioned with her chin for him to pull the stretcher holding the elderly gentleman back into the small bungalow. "I think we have company."

She'd closed the ambulance's door, but in this quiet retiree neighborhood, locking it hadn't seemed necessary. Before her partner could ask more questions, she whispered a quick prayer for protection, slipped out and padded toward the rig. Protocol demanded that a paramedic call the police if she feared for her safety, a practice she'd been a stickler about ever since her former partner had gotten himself killed, but the last thing she needed on her record was a nuisance cry-wolf call if it turned out to be nothing more than a curious kid inside. Maybe one of the neighbors' grandkids. Or worse. No one at all.

Her finger tensed over the radio's call button. She'd take a quick peek and if she saw anyone over four-six, she'd call it in.

"Get back in here with the patient and let *me* look," her partner hissed from the bungalow.

She put her finger to her lips and waved him off as she melted against the side of the ambulance to shield herself from the view of whoever was inside. The guys would never let her live it down if she turned tail and it turned out to be nothing. *Please, God, let it be nothing.*

The hair on the back of her neck prickled. Someone was *definitely* in there. She drew in a deep breath and glanced through the opening.

A lanky teen with unnaturally black hair stood at the wall-mounted cabinet, jabbing at the lock with a screwdriver. He slammed his fist into the steel and cursed.

Sherri jerked back out of sight and fumbled with the button on her radio. That was no curious grandkid.

The next instant she was yanked off her feet and hauled inside the truck. The kid spun her around and pinned her to the wall, the butt of his hand crushing her larynx. Drug-crazed eyes locked with hers. "Open it!"

"Okay," she mouthed, unable to get a breath past the pressure on her throat.

He slowly eased his hold, looking as if he wasn't sure he trusted her. His heavy-lidded, gauzy blue eyes seemed vaguely familiar, which shouldn't have surprised her in a town the size of Stalwart, Washington. But it rattled her more than ever. Maybe someone really was behind the bad things that only seemed to happen on her shift.

He shoved her toward the cabinet.

Making a show of thumbing through her keys, she depressed the call button on the radio and spoke as loudly and clearly as she could make her quaking voice cooperate. "We don't carry narcotics on board the ambulance."

"You're lying!"

At least he didn't seem to know that the four vials of morphine she carried for patients with extreme pain were on her person at all times. And she didn't dare tell him that the rest of the good drugs were in the trauma bag, still with her partner and the patient inside the house. The last thing she wanted to do was give their hip-fracture patient a heart attack.

With any luck this kid was crashing so fast that in another few minutes he wouldn't be able to put two and two together. By now her partner would have called the cavalry. She just had to keep the kid from going ballistic on her until they got here.

He grabbed her ponytail, twisted it mercilessly, and shoved her face into the cabinet. "Open it!"

Pain ripped through her scalp, exploded in her nose. Screaming, she rammed her boot heel into his kneecap.

He doubled over with a roar, but the grip on her hair only intensified.

Gritting her teeth against the torturous pull, she jabbed the keys between her fingers and swung. Her fist connected with his cheek.

Her partner charged up to the open side door. "Let her go!"

With lightning speed, the kid maneuvered her in front of him like a human shield. His arm tightened around her throat as he snapped open a switchblade. "Stay back!"

Dan, her six-foot, barrel-chested, former-army-medic partner, came to a dead halt at the foot of the door. His arms shot up, patted the air. "Okay, kid. Take it easy."

Straining to pull in a full breath, Sherri stopped struggling.

Blessed sirens split the air, the sound screaming closer. But the sound made the kid shaky. Real shaky. "Tell them to stay back or I'll cut her. I swear I'll cut her."

A whimper escaped her throat as she winged a desperate plea heavenward.

"Look at me," Dan said in a soothing tone. "You *don't* want to do this."

"Don't tell me what I want," her captor seethed, pricking the tip of the knife into her cheek. "Nobody cares what I want."

A sheriff's deputy stepped in front of her partner. "I care."

The kid's hold on her neck loosened a fraction, and Sherri dared to breathe.

"You don't care. You left." The teen's arm around her neck went rigid again, his knife poised dangerously close to her carotid. "You left and didn't come back!"

The deputy pulled his stun gun and painted the teen's shoulder with the laser beam. "Drop the knife and let her go, Eddie."

"Or what? You'd shoot your own brother?"

Sherri's heart jolted. *This was his brother?*

The deputy's arm wavered. "I can't let you hurt Sherri. You know that."

Something about the way he said her name sounded achingly familiar.

His tortured gaze flicked her way, sending an unexpected flutter through her chest.

She gasped. "Cole?" When had he gotten back to town? Become a cop?

He winced at her breathless question and didn't meet her eyes.

She hadn't seen him since he'd left for college seven years ago. And never came back.

Not once. Not to see his brother. Not to see his father. And definitely not to see the three-years-his-junior neighbor girl who'd been nursing a colossal secret crush on him.

Eddie's hold around her neck eased mercifully, but Sherri still struggled to pull in a full breath as her gaze clung to Cole. He was as tall as she remembered. But his brown hair was shorter and a shade darker. His chest broader. His voice deeper. And his eyes…

Those soft gray eyes that had once sparkled with mischievous teasing now brimmed with a tangle of apology, regret and despair.

She swallowed a rush of emotion.

"I wasn't going to hurt nobody," Eddie muttered, gesturing toward the cabinet with his knife. "He said the stuff was in here. Said it would be easy to lift."

Cole edged closer, his stun gun still fixed on his brother's shoulder, dangerously close to her own. "Who said?"

"The guy. *The guy!*" Eddie waved his knife as if Cole should know.

"Drop the knife, Eddie."

"I just needed a fix."

"I know." That telltale muscle twitch in Cole's

cheek gave her an odd pang of reassurance. "But I can't help you if you don't drop the knife."

"You don't wanna help me!" Eddie shoved her into Cole's line of fire and broke toward the rear door.

Thrown off balance, she tumbled out the side opening, right into Cole's arms. They closed protectively around her, his legs already in motion. And for a few blissful seconds she felt fifteen again. He rushed her away from the ambulance and coaxed her onto a porch step.

Her patient's porch step.

Remembering the poor gentleman who'd been in so much pain when they arrived, she lurched to her feet. "We need to transport our patient."

Cole urged her back down. "It's okay. Another ambulance is en route." He tucked a strand of hair behind her ear, the tenderness in his gaze making it difficult to breathe.

She forced herself to inhale a deep breath, but with it came his distinctive, spicy scent. A scent that had whisked her into silly happily-ever-after fantasies more times than she cared to remember. Memories assaulted her of the sweet kiss and soul-stirring hug they'd shared after she'd played paramedic and treated the swollen, bloodied knuckles he'd gotten taking out his anger on the wooden fence between their yards. She squeezed her eyes shut. She couldn't let him inside her head again and definitely not her heart.

At a sudden painful pressure against her cheek, she jerked back, her eyes popping open.

Cole's lips dipped into an apologetic frown. "Your cheek is bleeding." He held out a blood-stained tissue.

She accepted it from him and pressed it to the wound, cringing at what a wreck she must look. What was she supposed to say? *Good to see you after all these years.* Swallowing the lump in her throat, she settled for, "Thank you for getting me out in one piece."

He cradled her jaw in his palm and coaxed the muscles to relax with a soothing brush of his thumb. "You were amazing back there."

She stiffened, not wanting to acknowledge how something inside her came alive at his touch, at the admiration in his gaze.

Dan hurried toward her, trauma bag in hand.

But Cole didn't budge. "I'm sorry," he whispered, and she had the uncomfortable feeling he was apologizing for a lot more than his out-of-control brother.

If Cole needed any more proof that he shouldn't get involved in a serious relationship, he was staring her right in the face—sun-kissed hair pulled back in a ponytail, save for the wayward strands shielding wary blue eyes; trembling lips that even tipped down still dented her cheeks with those adorable dimples he used to lie awake thinking about; and that sweet strawberry scent that would forever transport him back to the day he'd stolen a kiss and she'd responded with a hug so touching it had probably kept him from doing something really stupid seven years ago—it and her admonition not to lose faith. Sherri Steele. The epitome of what his messed-up family had cost him.

She'd been the bright spot in their neighborhood, always quick to offer a smile or lend a hand.

Now, with another paramedic examining her neck, thanks to his brother's ruthless attack, she couldn't even look at him.

Exhaling, Cole tore his gaze from the purple smudges blooming under her eyes and turned to his partner, who was hauling his handcuffed brother off the sidewalk.

"This is your fault!" Eddie screamed, wrestling against Zeke's hold as he hurled increasingly colorful insults at Cole, his expression rabid.

This was *not* how Cole had hoped his first shift with the Stalwart Sheriff's Department would go down. Let alone his first meeting with Eddie. He'd anticipated needing the full armor of God to battle Eddie's inevitable resistance, *not* his stun gun. He'd been away seven years too long. Seven years of trying to convince himself that he wasn't his brother's keeper. Seven years of running from God. He tried not to cringe at Eddie's hollowed-out cheeks, heavy-lidded bloodshot eyes, the rat's nest of jet-black hair—not his natural color. Taking another deep breath, Cole bit back the lecture scraping his throat.

His brother was in no condition to hear it. And he had no right to say anything. If he wanted Eddie to listen to him, he needed to start by earning back his trust.

"He's tripping out pretty good," Cole said to his partner, who'd finally got Eddie subdued. "We'll need to take him to the hospital before we book him."

The balding heavyweight who'd bellowed at the sheriff for being "saddled with breaking Cole into the way things worked in Stalwart" propelled Eddie toward their cruiser. "Family connections will not get you any special treatment from me," Zeke hissed in Eddie's ear, shoving him hard against the trunk and digging a knee into Eddie's bony thigh as he reached for the rear door handle.

Cole started toward him, but then stopped himself. The manhandling was over-the-top, but if he stepped in Zeke would accuse him of favoritism. He'd already made it clear that he didn't appreciate Cole "usurping" the position that should have been his nephew's. Cole should've known the ornery deputy would try any tactic to prove

Cole didn't deserve to be here. Three years with the Seattle PD clearly didn't rank higher than blood with him. Talk about favoritism. As Zeke clamped his meaty palm on Eddie's head and pushed him into the backseat of the cruiser, Cole hoped his brother wouldn't add his silence to the list of things he held against him.

He should've made more effort to connect since he'd returned to town two days ago, considering it was the only reason he'd taken the job in the first place. Never mind the dozen calls he'd made to Eddie's cell phone. In this condition, his brother probably hadn't even known he was ignoring them. Cole should've dropped by the house. And if he'd had to face his father, well… so be it.

He wondered if Sherri still lived next door. She hadn't seemed to recognize Eddie, so she'd probably moved away before the dye job and downward spiral. If not for the call from an old high school buddy alerting him to the situation here, Cole might not have recognized Eddie at first glance, either.

"Did you hear me?" Zeke rounded the hood of the car.

"What?"

"I said did you get the paramedic's statement?"

Cole blinked, glanced back at Sherri, now being helped to her feet by her partner. She'd pulled the elastic from her hair, leaving it to tumble in soft sandy waves over her shoulders. She was more beautiful than he remembered. Of course, the last time he'd seen her she'd been only fifteen—just a girl. To an eighteen-year-old, the three-year age difference had seemed unbridgeable.

"Cole?" Zeke repeated gruffly.

"Not yet." He pulled his notebook from his pocket and headed toward Sherri, hating how scattered and unprofessional he was coming off. He couldn't have made a worse first impression if he'd tried.

And Zeke's griping about how his nephew wouldn't have forgotten wasn't helping.

The second ambulance had arrived. As Sherri's partner briefed the paramedics on the patient awaiting transport, Cole cut her away from the group. "I need to ask you a few questions for the report."

Her answering smile looked more like a wince. "It kind of hurts to talk."

His chest tightened. If he'd just manned up and gone to Dad's place the day he'd pulled into town, he might have averted this whole incident. "You really were amazing back there. Held it together when most people would've freaked."

Once again the compliment seemed to make her uncomfortable, or maybe it was him. Her gaze flitted from her partner to the police cruiser to the vicinity of his chin. "Would you have zapped him?"

"In a heartbeat. If I'd had a clear shot."

Anguish flickered in her eyes, reminding him of the caring girl who'd nursed back to health every injured creature he'd brought to her doorstep.

He reached for her hand as naturally as she'd reached for his the day he'd been the injured creature on her doorstep. Her fingers felt like ice and remained coolly rigid. "I love my brother, Sherri. But your welfare comes first."

Her surprised gaze jumped to his.

"I'm not going to stand by and do nothing while he hurts innocent people," he added, needing to convince her for a reason he didn't want to examine too closely.

Her gaze dove back to the sidewalk as her hand slipped from his grasp.

Her retreat hurt more than it should have, considering she'd just been ambushed by his brother.

"Listen, I can come by the ambulance base later to get your statement. But I need to confirm a couple of things. Eddie took you hostage to coerce you into handing over narcotics?"

"Not at first. I surprised him when—" grimacing, she splayed her fingers over her throat and sank back to the porch step "—when he was trying to break into the cabinet."

"Okay." He hated to press her for details when talking was obviously painful. But… "One more question for now. Do you have any idea who the guy he referred to is?"

She shook her head.

Cole pocketed his notebook and hunkered down in front of her until she couldn't help but look at him. "I'll make sure Eddie never bothers you again. I promise." The disbelief that flickered in her eyes at her nod pierced clean through his soul. "I'm sorry this happened."

"Fat lot of good sorry does her," her partner growled, stalking toward them. "You need to lock that punk up and throw away the key. He's done nothing but terrorize Sherri for weeks!"

"What?" Cole's heart couldn't have jolted harder if the guy had slapped paddles on his chest and zapped him. He jerked his attention back to Sherri. "Is that true?"

She shook her head repeatedly this time.

"*Someone's* doing it," her partner hissed.

"Whoa, whoa. Back up a second." Cole pulled out his notebook again. "These incidents, were they reported?"

"No, they've been little things. The kind of things that could happen to any paramedic. Crank calls. Getting sideswiped." He motioned toward Sherri's black eye. "Assaults."

"So what makes you think that Eddie's behind them? They all sound pretty random."

"'Cause they only happen to her!"

The color drained from Sherri's face, her white cheeks a sickeningly stark contrast to the bruises around her eyes and throat. "Dan, leave it alone," she whispered.

Cole's heart lurched. She was afraid. Anyone with two eyes could see it. So why didn't she want the incidents investigated? Did she know who was behind the other attacks?

Dan shot a scowl toward the rear window of the cruiser. "A kid like that doesn't hang around a neighborhood like this. No way did he just *happen* upon our ambulance. Not unless he's breaking into old folks' houses to grab their prescription meds." His lips curled menacingly. "Either way, he needs to be locked up."

"No argument here," Zeke agreed, his rear resting on the cruiser's hood, his legs stretched casually in front of him, his arms crossed.

Cole ignored him, focusing instead on Sherri as he clasped her elbow. "When I come by I'll want details on every suspicious incident." Her trembling reverberated through him, sending way too many unwelcome scenarios bouncing around his brain.

Her lips flattened into a silent line, and she stepped backward toward her truck.

"Okay?" he pressed. "I want to help you get to the bottom of what's going on."

Zeke snorted. "Why don't you start by barking up your own family tree?"

Sherri wrapped her arms tightly around her middle and shook her head. "It's not your problem, Cole."

"I'm making it my problem."

TWO

"What am I going to do with you?" Sherri's boss rested his hip on the corner of his cluttered desk. "Every time I turn around you're getting into trouble."

The rain that had started soon after Eddie's attack now pelted the office window as fast and furiously as her heart pinging her ribs. The ambulance base was a three-strike operation. Not that any of the incidents that had happened to her lately could really be called strikes, no matter how much her boss liked to intimate as much. Yes, she'd left the ambulance unlocked, but not one of their paramedics would have thought twice about leaving it unlocked in that neighborhood. "I'm sorry, sir," she said.

"I'd like you to take a few days off."

"That's not necessary." The last thing she wanted was free time. The busier she kept, the less time she had to think. To relive her dead partner's shooting. She swallowed and caught herself

wincing at the pain still plaguing her throat cour-
tesy of Eddie's stranglehold. "I'm fine. Really."
Or she would be if she could shut out the memory
of Cole's concerned gaze searching hers and his
husky declaration that he was making *her* problem *his* problem.

"*You* may be fine," her boss scolded, "but the
station's morale has hit rock bottom. One more
incident like this and no one's going to want to
work with you. You know what they call you?"

"Yes, sir." She lifted her chin. Princess Dark
Cloud was actually a step up from what they used
to call her—Ice Queen.

He studied her in silence for an unnervingly
long moment. "Your partner Dan has convinced
one of the sheriff's deputies that the incidents
haven't been merely unlucky coincidences. Is that
what you think?"

Sherri pressed her sweaty palms against her
navy blue slacks, debating her response. Her boss
wouldn't want to hear what she really thought.
But she heard the way her fellow officers still
whispered about the shooting when they thought
she wasn't around. They blamed her for letting
Luke die. They didn't want her here and would
do just about anything to drive her to quit. She
was sure of it. But she was just as sure that God
had let her survive for a reason.

She curled her fingers into fists. "I don't know

what to think, sir. But I assure you I can handle whatever curveballs are thrown at me." Because there was no way she'd let Luke down a second time.

"Unfortunately, some of those curveballs are turning into boomerangs that are beating us up-side the head."

Tension hummed along her nerves. "Pardon me?"

"Reinhart, the widower whose wife died of a heart attack last month, is demanding an inquest. Claims your refusal to come up to his apartment without a police escort cost too many minutes. Minutes that could've saved his wife."

"Sir, I'm deeply sorry for his loss, but the building was flagged for multiple drug-related incidents. I followed protocol."

"Yes," he said, but didn't sound pleased about it. No doubt thinking if it hadn't been her in that ambulance, he wouldn't be facing an inquest.

"Any paramedic would have done the same. Did Dan say otherwise?" The men liked to be cowboys, but she'd thought they'd learned their lesson after what had happened to Luke. If she and Luke had followed protocol that morning, he might still be alive. Her chest tightened at thoughts of other choices that might have kept him alive.

Her boss shrugged. "Not in so many words."

A rap on the door made her jump, but not nearly as fitfully as her insides trampolined when Cole stepped into view.

His gaze narrowed in on her cheek and his eyes darkened.

She finger-combed her hair over the butterfly bandage binding the cut his brother had given her.

"You must be Donovan." Her boss beckoned Cole in. "You can use my office to question Sherri. Her shift is covered, so take as long as you need."

Sherri nodded, straining to appear cooperative when everything inside her wanted to bolt.

He stepped through the door, and the room seemed to shrink, much like the crisply ironed shirt straining at his muscular shoulders.

She looked away, not wanting to notice how good he looked in a uniform. Not wanting to imagine that concern *for her* had etched those creases into his brow.

He might say her welfare came first, but she'd stopped believing in fairy tales long ago. Never mind how princelike he'd seemed today. He'd do the same for any innocent person. He was here to question her about the incidents, *not* to get reacquainted.

The sooner she told him what he wanted to know, the sooner he'd be on his way.

As her boss stepped out of the room, she sank

into a chair and grasped for a light tone. "You're his dream come true. If everything that's happened goes on the record, he'll claim I should be put on administrative leave *for my own safety* until you can figure out who's behind everything."

"Sounds like a smart move to me."

"No," she said firmly. "It's not."

His eyebrow arched curiously. "Why's that?"

She tapped her fingers to her lips, fighting to rein in her galloping pulse. She couldn't tell him that her days off were worse. That she'd rather fight off a drug-crazed kid than— She cut off the thought and casually slid her fingers from her mouth to tame an invisible strand of wayward hair. "Because I need every shift I can get if I'm going to qualify for the next flight medic job that opens up," she improvised with the same story she'd used on her parents to justify taking extra shifts. Once she got the flight medic job, things would get better. There wouldn't be so many reminders.

Cole smiled, the corners of his eyes crinkling in that way that used to make her heart flutter.

She silently groaned at the realization that it still did.

"A flight medic, wow! I can't help feeling a little proud that you took my advice."

The warmth in his voice did funny things to

her insides. That and the fact he remembered his murmured, "You'd make a good paramedic," that day she'd treated his swollen knuckles.

"It's good to see you doing so well."

She pasted on a smile and nodded. "So what brings you back to Stalwart?" She glanced at his left hand, but his fingers were tucked out of sight. "You married? Come back to settle down?" Her cheeks heated. Why on earth had she asked him that?

His gaze darkened. "No, working law enforcement and marriage aren't a good mix."

"Hah," she scoffed. "I have several happily married uncles and cousins who would loudly disagree."

"Appearances can be deceptive."

Resisting the urge to massage her bruised throat, she sat up straighter. Yeah, she knew all about keeping up appearances. "Then you'll understand why I don't want these incidents blown out of proportion. Because, between you and me, I'm pretty sure I'm just being hazed."

"Hazed?" Cole's eyes widened. "But you've already been on the job a couple of years. Haven't you?"

"Almost three." She pressed her lips together, wishing she'd kept her mouth shut. Hazing had seemed like an innocuous way to say her colleagues didn't want to work with her.

Cole studied her too intently as he pulled a notepad and pencil from his shirt pocket. "How about you tell me what you remember about each incident?"

She exhaled, relieved that at least he hadn't pressed for reasons for her hazing suspicions. "I'm not convinced they can be called *incidents*. Dan is overreacting. Nothing has happened to me that hasn't happened to any other paramedic at one time or another."

"Difference is they keep happening to you."

Yeah, okay. There was that. "They were incidental things like being called to an address that didn't exist or being propositioned by a half-doped patient who claimed he'd never called an ambulance."

Cole flinched as if the thought of some creep pawing her made him feel sick.

"Nothing I couldn't handle," she stressed, trying not to squirm under the intensity of his troubled gaze. The reaction of the other paramedics, who'd slapped her on the back and complimented the Ice Queen for kneeing the loser in the groin, had been easier to handle. Ironically, their hazing probably had helped her tough it out when she'd felt like quitting as much as they wanted her to.

"When did the incidents start?"

"I can't say for sure." The whispering had started first. Luke's death had been the tipping point for her colleagues. He'd been a good man, a true friend. And the only paramedic who hadn't griped about teaming with her after she'd gotten her first partner fired for drinking on the job.

"You did the right thing," he'd said the first time they'd driven to a call together. He hadn't said what he was referring to. Hadn't needed to. She wasn't sure if he'd ever known how much those five little words had meant to her, because they'd never talked about it again.

"Sherri?"

She jerked her attention back to Cole. "Um."

"Can you give me dates, addresses, descriptions?"

She stared at Cole, taking a moment to register his question. "I'd have to pull out my reports."

"Are they handy?"

She rolled her eyes.

"Okay, we'll worry about that later."

No, there couldn't be any *later*. With Eddie's attack, her boss's innuendoes and Cole's unexpected charge back into her life, she was scarcely handling *now*. She pushed to her feet. "Just a second and I'll grab them." As she tugged the coil-bound book from the top shelf of her locker, her Bible toppled to the floor, spilling a month's worth of church bulletins and inserts at her feet.

She quickly stuffed all but one back into her locker and rejoined Cole in her boss's office.

Handing Cole the pamphlet for Teen Challenge, a faith-based residential program that helped young men and women overcome addictions, she said, "I found this while I was grabbing my call journal and thought it might be something you'd want to look into for Eddie. Some of the men that are in the program spoke at our church last week. It's turned their lives around. If you could convince Eddie to go—"

"I don't want to send him away," Cole said gruffly. He glanced at the pamphlet then slipped it into the back of his notebook. "I appreciate the suggestion," he added, his tone gentler this time. "Helping him is the reason I came back to Stalwart."

Of course it was. Sherri glanced away, focused on the world outside, blurred by the rain streaming down the window. In the months after he'd left, her imagination had read too much into his surprise parting gift, let alone the gratitude that had been in his eyes after that world-tilting hug. But when months turned into years, the truth eventually had sunk in. Not that it would matter anymore now. She couldn't afford to let anyone get close.

"If I'd been here for Eddie in the first place…" Cole continued, but then shook his head and motioned to her call journal. "Tell me about the other incidents."

She skimmed the entries and offered several examples, a few of which she had to admit that even she couldn't see the guys pulling. She closed her journal. A lot of them may have been purely random occurrences.

Cole looked up from his notepad. "Is that all of them? Your partner mentioned your ambulance being hit."

She frowned. "That couldn't have been deliberate."

"Where your safety is concerned, I don't want to take any chances."

She gulped at the determination blazing in his eyes. Did he mean *her* safety in particular?

Bothered that she cared one way or the other, she glanced away. She just wasn't used to having an ally in her corner, at least not at work. Her family was great, but between the veteran firefighters and deputy-sheriff cousins and uncles, she preferred not to talk shop around them.

"Tell me about the accident," Cole prodded.

"Oh, right. Um, it happened last week. A pickup sideswiped our ambulance as we turned on to County Road 15. There's a police report on that one."

"Did they arrest the driver?"

"No. The pickup was stolen. They found it abandoned down the road."

"Did you get a look at the driver?"

For the first time she realized what Cole was really asking, had been trying to get at all along—could this guy have been his brother? This wasn't about her at all. Not really.

"Sherri?"

"No, I didn't." She squinted at the window, picturing that night. "He was wearing a hoodie. That's all I remember." Was it any wonder the driver hadn't seen her turning off the side road with his hood up like that? The collision couldn't have been deliberate.

"Were you hurt?"

Cole's anxious tone didn't help her churning stomach, but she managed to shrug as if it was all in a day's work.

He looked over his notes, his eyes as stormy as the sky. "Can you think of any reason why someone would target you?"

I let my partner die. She didn't say it, just shrugged again.

"A patient or maybe a family member of a patient who blames you for a death?"

She gasped.

"I take it you've thought of someone?"

"Rolph Reinhart has demanded an inquest into his wife's death due to delay in treatment. But he's over eighty years old. I can't see him doing any of—" she motioned to the notebook he was writing in "—those things."

"I'll talk to him. Can you think of anyone else?"

She racked her brain, flipped through her call journal. "No, no one." For the most part she'd been fortunate with outcomes. Not like Luke who'd been threatened by a shooting victim's fellow gang members when the victim hadn't survived. They'd claimed Luke was tight with their rival gang and had deliberately let their man die.

"How about a jealous ex-boyfriend?"

She snorted. "No." She'd broken up with a guy or two over the years, but none had ever caused trouble.

"A rival then? Maybe a woman who—?"

"No."

He squinted at her, clearly perturbed by her certainty. "Your fellow paramedics are not behind these incidents, Sherri. Your partner was the one who urged me to investigate."

"Could've been to throw off suspicions."

"You obviously didn't see his face as he treated that cut on your cheek." Cole grazed his fingers across the hair she'd nudged over the bandage.

She inhaled reflexively.

Big mistake. With him so close, she could smell the spicy scent that instantly transported her back to her sophomore year—and the dreamy guy living next door.

"Why are you so convinced your coworkers are behind these incidents?"

She sprang from her chair and walked to the window, regretting that she'd said anything. Out on the street a woman fought to right her umbrella, turned inside out by the wind. Sherri could so relate. Dan's protective outburst had been out of character, but maybe the guys had merely opted to try another tactic to derail her. "Do you think Dan would've asked the police to investigate if these incidents had happened to him or one of the other guys?"

Cole didn't respond for a long time.

She sneaked a peek over her shoulder at him.

He, too, was watching the woman wrestling with her umbrella. "You think it's because you're a woman that they're trying to scare you into quitting?"

She let out a humorless laugh. *Close enough.* "You've got to admit that it's a lot more palatable than thinking some faceless stalker is after me."

"But what if you're wrong?"

The next night Sherri's "faceless stalker" comment was still replaying in Cole's head as the compulsion to stick close to the ambulance base and keep an eye on her warred with the need to visit his brother.

He didn't blame Eddie for refusing to talk to him yesterday after the way he'd let Zeke manhandle him. He probably should've bailed him out of jail himself instead of leaving it to their father, but he'd hoped the brief taste of life behind bars would scare him straight.

Cole slid into his truck and stared at the drug rehab pamphlet Sherri had pressed on him yesterday, still a little stunned that she'd been more concerned with getting his brother help than fretting over her own situation. It had physically hurt to look at her black eye and the cut his brother had sliced in her cheek. The least he could do for her was get to the truth about the suspicious incidents on her shifts.

Reinhart was definitely out as a suspect. The man was on oxygen 24/7, but he had a son, a son Cole had yet to catch up with. As for Sherri's suspicions of her colleagues, he hadn't gotten the sense from any of the other paramedics that they resented her or had any other reason to haze her.

Then again, besides her partner, no one he'd interviewed had seemed concerned that the rash of incidents involving her was anything more than coincidence. Even her uncle, a sergeant in the department, hadn't known about them until Cole mentioned them. Apparently, Sherri hadn't breathed a word about the incidents to her family.

Cole tucked the pamphlet she'd shared into his glove box. He wasn't surprised that her uncle couldn't imagine anyone having a reason to deliberately target someone as caring as Sherri. Eddie certainly didn't have one.

At least no reason that Cole knew of. But he didn't really know his brother anymore. Which was what he'd come to town to change. Cole started his truck and headed toward the old family home. He'd let himself get sidetracked long enough.

As he turned on to their street, Cole's palms started to sweat. He hadn't faced his dad in seven years and wouldn't today if he could avoid it. He parked his truck a few houses shy of the driveway so he could slip out the back if Dad made it an early night with whatever woman he was dating these days. He shrank back at sight of Sherri's parents exiting the neighboring house. He waited until they'd locked up and driven off, then hurried past.

From the corner of his dad's lot, Cole cut across the lawn, expecting to kick up clouds of dandelion fluff with every step. But under the forgiving cover of twilight, the place looked surprisingly tidy.

Maybe Eddie's arrest had drummed some responsibility into Dad. The TV flicked on in the living room, and Dad settled on the couch. Alone. No date.

Cole clasped the porch stair rail. The green paint crumbled off in his hand and an odd sadness twisted in his chest. Painting the rails had been his and dad's spring project for as long as he could remember. That and tinkering on the old Camaro.

Bypassing the porch for the moment, Cole rounded the corner of the house to peek in the garage. He rubbed a clear circle in the dingy window. The Camaro was still there. He wondered if Dad ever worked on it with Eddie.

Being the youngest, Eddie had always been more of a mama's boy, which was probably why it'd almost killed Mom when he'd chosen to stay in Stalwart with Dad. Cole couldn't blame Eddie for not wanting to leave his friends, but if he'd heard how Mom had cried herself to sleep every night, maybe he wouldn't have minded making new friends.

The ones he had here sure hadn't done him any favors.

At the sound of a bedroom window sliding open, Cole ducked behind the hedges that hugged the base of the house and the memory of a much younger Sherri playing hide and seek in his yard whispered through his mind. As an only child eager to join in their games, she'd helped bridge the wide age gap between him and his brother on lazy summer afternoons. A backpack thumped the dirt under the window. Then, clad in a black hoodie, Eddie perched on the window ledge of the darkened room.

Cole's temper flared. Eddie wasn't supposed to be out after dark—a too-little-too-late curfew had been imposed by Dad, who clearly wasn't paying any better attention to what his youngest son was up to than he had before Eddie's arrest. As his brother jumped to the ground, Cole resisted the urge to read Eddie the riot act here and now, opting instead to see where he headed.

Eddie darted behind the garage and re-emerged a second later pedaling his bike.

Cole waited until he'd turned onto the street and had gotten a few houses ahead before he jogged back to his truck. When Eddie reached the corner, Cole pulled his vehicle onto the street at a crawl. This could be the break he'd been hoping for. Eddie had refused to snitch on his drug sources, but something told him his little brother was about to lead him straight to them.

Eddie crossed street after street heading toward the west side of town, seemingly oblivious to Cole's truck trailing a block behind him. Halfway up Belmont, Eddie ramped the curb and swerved to the back of a squat bungalow.

Parking in front of the playground a few houses shy of Eddie's destination, Cole's internal radar ratcheted to high alert. The neighborhood was one of the older ones in town. The postage-stamp lawns appeared neatly kept for the most part. But it didn't take his brother showing up here to tell him something about the neighborhood wasn't right. It was a Friday night, and the streetlights hadn't kicked on; yet, there wasn't a kid to be seen.

Cole quickly circled to the far end of the playground where soccer fields bordered the backs of the houses for the rest of the street. A discarded cold medicine package caught in the fence reinforced his suspicions that the guy Eddie came to see was a drug dealer. If he'd been driving his cruiser, he could've checked the system to see if they'd had any recent trouble in the area.

As he sprinted to the back of the house Eddie had targeted, the wail of a distant ambulance roused concerns for Sherri. But he couldn't trail her ambulance, let alone do a thing to protect her until he got his brother out of here.

Peering past the detached garage between him and the house, Cole spotted Eddie picking his way up the back steps of the dimly lit bungalow. Its blinds were drawn, and Cole had no illusions the owner would welcome his arrival.

The wood of the dilapidated veranda groaned under Eddie's weight.

Gripping the chain-link fence, Cole scrutinized the backyard for booby traps. Drug dealers could be sickly creative about safeguarding their privacy.

The veranda's wooden floor suddenly cracked, and Eddie dropped out of sight, yelping like a whipped pup.

"Eddie?" Cole hissed.

A low groan rose from below the porch.

With one last visual sweep of the backyard, Cole vaulted over the fence. Monitoring the windows for signs of movement inside, he edged toward the house.

Eddie's head bobbed above the splintered wood.

"What were you thinking?" Cole hissed, offering him a hand out.

Eddie startled at Cole's hand in his face, but a burst of light from a nearby window got him moving. As he cleared the rotted floorboard, a pill bottle tumbled from his pocket.

Cole confiscated the drugs and stuffed them into his jeans pocket.

"Hey, that's mine!"

"Only if you want to land yourself back in jail."

At the scrape of the door's dead bolt, Cole yanked Eddie into the shadow of a nearby bush. A second later the door cracked open.

From his vantage point, Cole couldn't make out anything more than the guy was over six feet and had a pistol clamped in his fist.

He hovered in the doorway a long moment, his pistol aimed at the hole in the porch floor, then pulled the door shut again.

As the dead bolt clicked once more, Cole caught sight of Eddie's bike propped against the side of the garage. No way had the man missed it. Cole dug his fingers into the fabric of Eddie's hoodie. "We've got to get out of here, now." Then, he'd worry about figuring out a way to shut this place down. One that wouldn't land his brother in jail.

Or worse, on the wrong end of a vindictive drug dealer's gun.

Eddie whirled the opposite direction. "My bike."

Cole tightened his grip. "Forget the bike." He hauled him across the driveway, scarcely giving him time to keep his feet under him, and plunged into the cover of the hedge edging the property.

Eddie slapped branches from his face. "What are you doing here?"

"Saving your hide. Now move." He gritted his teeth to hold back a lecture. He intended to give it, but first he needed to put a good mile between Eddie and this place. Finding a sparse section, he shoved Eddie through the bushes into the next yard. "My truck's at the park."

The wailing ambulance he'd somehow stopped hearing blasted around the corner and braked at the foot of the driveway. At the sight of Sherri jumping from the passenger side, his heart lurched. He dug out his keys and slapped them into Eddie's hand. "Wait for me in the truck."

By the time Cole pushed back through the hedge, Dan and Sherri were rolling a gurney toward the drug dealer's front door. "Wait!"

Motion-detector lights flicked on, exposing a suspicious mass in the branches of the tree in front of the house.

"Get down!"

THREE

Sherri dove to the dirt, scarcely escaping the giant feedbag that swung off a branch. The sack caught Dan in the back and sent him crashing against the gurney, which pitched onto her and punched the breath from her lungs.

Cole tore the gurney off her and propped it on its edge like a shield between them and the house. "You okay?"

A pleasant sensation fluttered through her chest at his protective presence. "Now I am." She army-crawled toward her groaning partner.

"I'm fine." Dan pushed her hand away. "Just give me a second to catch my breath."

Cole pointed to the trip wire Dan's foot must've caught. "You may not have a second! Get back to the ambulance. Both of you."

"The trauma bag." Sherri reached for it.

Cole ripped off the straps securing it to the stretcher and shoved it toward her. "Go," he barked, drawing a gun from his ankle holster.

Heart in her throat, she pushed to her feet alongside Dan and ran hunched over to the back of the ambulance.

As soon as they jumped inside, Cole rounded the rear door and called for backup. "The call. What was it for?"

Sherri snatched up her stethoscope to check Dan's lungs. "Asthma."

Cole squinted at Dan. "Are you up to transporting a patient if this call turns out to be legit?"

She fumbled the stethoscope. *Legit?* He thought the feedbag was meant for her.

"Yeah, I can drive." Dan stopped rubbing his chest and dropped his hand to his side. "Just got the wind knocked out of me. Good thing Sherri ducked when she did. It would've taken her head off."

Cole's strangled gasp left her own chest tight. That and the gun he had trained on the house.

Reflexively, her palms clapped over her ears, the shot that had ripped through Luke's chest blasting through her head. *Breathe. Cole's safe. Dan's safe.*

"You okay?" Concern edged Cole's voice. And the heart-in-his-eyes look he swept over her, as if he desperately needed reassurance she was truly unharmed, felt…nice. *Really nice.*

Slipping her hands from her ears, she forced her gaze away from the deadly steel in his hands to his attire—black jeans and T-shirt, not his deputy uniform. "What's going on? What are you doing here?"

The muscle in his cheek flinched and her stomach fluttered. Had he followed the ambulance to keep watch over her?

He slanted a glance down the street, then returned his full attention to the house, not her. "I was in the neighborhood."

Confused by his gruff response, she squinted through the deepening twilight at the truck parked at the curb a few houses away. His truck. And it had been there before they arrived. "How did you know about the trap?"

"Someone came out of the house," Dan hissed, peering out the window on the ambulance's side door.

Sherri squinted over her partner's shoulder as a dark figure disappeared into the detached garage. "What do we do now?"

With an intensity that knotted her stomach, Cole peered past the ambulance's back door he was using as cover.

"You can't go after him. Not without backup!"

A sheriff's cruiser whipped around the corner and careened to a stop behind the ambulance, silencing her objection. Cole flashed his ID. "We've got a booby-trapped property. One male in the garage. Unknown number in the house. Cover me."

Without waiting for a response, Cole snuck along the side of the house using bushes as cover.

Bushes! What good would a bush do him? It wouldn't stop a bullet. *Please, Lord, don't let another man get shot because of me.*

The sheriff's deputy hunched behind his cruiser, his gun pointed at the garage as he barked orders into the radio on his shoulder.

The garage door rumbled open, accompanied by the roar of an engine.

Cole darted closer.

"Look out," the deputy shouted as a motorcycle blasted from the garage and screamed away.

A deafening explosion blew out the windows of the house, rocking the ambulance.

"Cole!" Sherri shoved open the side door and sprang to the ground. Shielding her face from falling debris with her arm, she scanned the area she'd last seen him, except the explosion could have thrown him anywhere. Smoke stung her eyes as she silently pleaded with God to let her find him.

"There!" Dan jumped to the ground behind her and pointed to a dark shape on the far side of the driveway.

She sprinted toward him and scooped her arms under his armpits to pull him away from the fire.

"Through here." Dan helped her pull him through a scraggly section of hedge into the next yard, where she instantly dropped to her knees at his side.

"Cole, talk to me. Cole!"

The deputy ordered emerging neighbors back into their houses between demands into his radio for fire trucks and someone to catch the man on the motorcycle. "Is he okay?"

Sweat slicked her trembling hands. "I don't know. He's not responding." She forced herself to take deep breaths. *Oh, God, I can't have a panic attack. Not here. Not now.*

"Try a sternal rub," Dan ordered before dashing back to the ambulance.

Cole moaned at the pressure, but didn't open his eyes or answer her.

"Cole, tell me where you hurt."

Dan dropped the trauma bag beside her. "Anything?"

"He responded to pain, but isn't talking." Sherri checked his airway. "Airway clear." She slid her fingertips to his wrist as Dan pulled out a stethoscope. "Pulse a hundred twenty and strong."

She palpated his stomach and was rewarded with another groan. "Abdomen soft, no internals, yet. Cole, can you hear me?"

"He's got decreased breath sounds on the left side. Could be looking at a collapsed lung."

"How bad is that?" A kid skidded to his knees beside her.

Sherri's breath stalled in her throat. "Eddie? What are you—?"

Dan surged to his feet. "You again?" He grabbed Eddie's collar and hauled him away from her. "You made the call. Didn't you?"

Sherri's heart jumped to her throat. *Eddie had set her up?*

Dan shoved him up against the side of the cruiser. "What kind of sick—?"

"Hey, what are you doing?" The deputy rushed toward them.

"This punk attacked my partner yesterday trying to get drugs," Dan growled. "He's got to be behind this crank call, too."

"I'm not," Eddie cried. "You've gotta believe me!"

Disturbingly, Cole didn't react to Dan's accusations, didn't even open his eyes.

The deputy snapped open his handcuff pouch. "This true, ma'am?"

Ignoring the question, she raised Cole's left eyelid. "Cole, are you with me?"

Both eyes blinked open and a slow smile curved his lips. "Hi," he said softly, then sheer panic swept over his face.

"Cole? Dan, forget the kid. I need you here." She struggled to tamp down the alarm edging into her voice. "Cole, what's wrong?"

Dan shoved Eddie at the deputy. "Keep him away from her."

"I didn't do anything," the kid bellowed. "I need to stay with my brother."

Cole rolled to his side and tried to push himself up. "Let him go. He didn't—" His voice cut out on a frown.

"You need to lie still." Sherri exchanged a worried glance with Dan as he caught Cole's shoulder and compelled him to stay put.

Cole's gaze shifted to her lips, his forehead wrinkling. "I can't hear." He pressed the heel of his hand to his temple, his gaze bouncing from her to the commotion around them. "I can't hear anything."

She leaned over him so he'd see the reassurance in her face and maybe read her lips. "You need to lie still so we can help you." She flicked her penlight over his eyes. "Pupils round and reactive."

His gaze darted back to his brother.

She laid her palm on his pounding chest and waited until he looked at her, her own heart galloping at how vulnerable he looked lying there. "Eddie's fine." She stuffed down the silly disappointment that Cole hadn't been here for her as she'd first supposed.

"He's got a contusion on the side of the head,"

Dan reported. "No bleeding or fluid from the ears. Check for broken bones."

Mentally cataloging the serious injuries they could still be looking at, she continued her palpitations, her fingers trembling. "Breathe," she coached. He'd only been here because he'd been following his brother, not her. She wasn't to blame.

Not this time.

Below his hipbone, Sherri's fingers pressed into something hard. Probing it, she felt the distinctive shape of a prescription bottle. Glancing up, she found Eddie's gaze fixed on her hands and swallowed the bile rising in her throat. They'd been buying drugs?

Cole's hand locked on her wrist. "Please, don't," he whispered, a soul-deep pain shadowing his eyes.

Disappointment clutched her chest. He must've followed his brother here, confiscated the drugs Eddie had just bought. He wasn't helping Eddie by covering for him. But just like the silly teenager who'd have agreed to anything if it'd meant Cole would notice her, she couldn't say no. Was ignoring what she found the same as lying? Her heart seesawed in her chest, her gaze fixed on Cole's. His brother had held a knife to her throat. Only an idiot would keep this to herself. Eddie was a danger to himself and anyone who came between him and a fix.

"You find something?" Dan's voice cut into her thoughts.

She held Cole's gaze for a long moment. She couldn't *not* keep his secret. Not after he'd just saved her hide. No matter why he'd really been here. She tugged her wrist free of Cole's grasp and quickly palpated the rest of his leg. "No broken bones."

"Okay, our gurney's toast. I'll bring the ambulance around. We need to get it out of the way of the fire trucks anyway."

"I can walk," Cole said, his hearing apparently returning. He tried pushing himself to a sitting position with a frustrated groan.

She cupped his elbow to help him. "On a scale of one to ten, how bad's the pain?"

"Three," he said through gritted teeth.

She rolled her eyes. "I'll give you some meds anyway, tough guy."

"Thank you," he murmured.

Warmth surged through her and with it the memory of the last time he'd thanked her for nursing his wounds. His soft kiss. Her first. And the hug that neither of them had seemed to want to end. She'd relived that moment too many times to count in the seven years since. She blinked away the memory, cleared her throat. "Just doing my job."

He started to shake his head, winced at the movement. "I mean thank you for trusting me."

Her heart flip-flopped. He was talking about the drugs he'd asked her to keep secret. "I hope you know what you're doing."

Two days later, Cole walked into the sheriff's office, his head still throbbing along with his ribs, but at least his hearing was back to normal.

Or at least enough not to miss Zeke's gloating stage whisper to the deputy beside him that his nephew wouldn't have been off on sick leave less than a week into a new job. Cole pressed his fingertips to his forehead and temple, wondering how much of today's headache was due to the mild concussion the doctor said he'd suffered and how much from dreading this interview.

He'd had every intention of handing over the drugs he'd found on Eddie to the sheriff and explaining the situation. But that was before Sherri had showed up and everything had blown apart. He hadn't needed to hear what her partner had ranted to the deputy to know he figured Eddie had lured her there.

He had a bad feeling that whoever made the 9-1-1 call had deliberately set up Eddie. But who? And why? Questions he had hoped to have answers to by now. Cole sliced a glance at Zeke. The whole scenario had played nicely into his disgruntled partner's agenda, but…that didn't mean he'd set it up.

According to Eddie, the same guy who'd prodded him to raid Sherri's ambulance had given him the tip on the supposed great deal at the drug house—not Zeke. Trouble was Eddie still couldn't identify the guy.

The deputy who'd taken control of the scene outside the drug house motioned Cole to an interrogation room. "I figured you'd appreciate some privacy. Don't pay any attention to Zeke. Trust me, no one else wanted his nephew to get the job."

Taking a seat, Cole opted not to respond, since he had no idea who might be listening in on the other side of the two-way mirror.

I hope you know what you're doing. Sherri's words whispered through his mind for the hundredth time as the lanky deputy straddled a chair and laid a file folder on the table.

"Okay." The deputy tapped his pen against the folder. "Why don't you start by telling me why you were in the neighborhood?"

"I already told you." At least a half dozen times when the deputy had interrogated him in the hospital. "It's no secret that my brother's an addict. I spotted him sneaking out his bedroom window. Figured he was up to no good. Followed him to the drug house and yanked him out before he could make a buy."

"Did he stop at the variety store on the corner?"

Cole's insides jumped at the new question. "No."

The deputy studied him for an uncomfortably long minute. "You're sure?"

"Yes, why?"

"The 9-1-1 call that summoned the ambulance was made from a phone booth there."

The knots in Cole's neck eased at the confirmation that his brother couldn't have secretly made the call without Cole noticing. "I already told you he didn't make the call. Since when is a deputy's word not a reliable alibi?"

"You're his brother."

"Yeah, and I'm Sherri's friend." He winced at the memory of their argument in the ambulance on the way to the hospital. She'd been furious that he'd asked her to keep quiet about the pill bottle in his pocket. Or more accurately "to shelter Eddie from the consequences of his actions." Consequences that might get him the help he needed… or so she thought.

Never mind that the pill bottle had turned out to be an old codeine prescription of their father's. But yeah, the fact that Cole had asked her to conceal it a mere day after his brother had held a knife to her throat was testimony to how hard he'd smashed his head.

Any other woman would've been jumping at the chance to get Eddie off the streets. Except—Cole planted his elbow on the table and buried his fingers in his hair—with her hovering over him, those beautiful blue eyes filled with concern, he hadn't had a hope of thinking straight.

Worse than that, he'd asked her to compromise her principles.

"You okay?" the deputy asked.

Cole blinked. Massaged his forehead. "Yeah, sorry, still nursing a headache." And still nursing a seven-year-old infatuation that had started when Sherri found him pounding his fist into the fence that had separated their yards after he'd learned his father had been cheating on Mom.

Sherri had dabbed antiseptic on his grazed knuckles, and he remembered feeling as if just by allowing her to help him, he'd been sullying her somehow, tainting her innocence by exposing her to his family's mixed-up morality.

Seven years later nothing had changed. Same girl. Same infatuation. Same insurmountable obstacle of his family.

Cole glanced at the clock on the wall behind the deputy and wondered if Dad was keeping a better eye on Eddie today. As much as he would have liked to avoid his dad, he'd had no choice but to allow Dad to visit him in the hospital to warn him about the prescription Eddie had stolen on top of sneaking out of the house to buy more drugs. The fact that Dad had seen the conversation as an invitation to pick up where'd they'd left off the day before his selfishness blew apart their family was proof of how mixed up his morality was.

But if you do not forgive others their sins, your Father will not forgive your sins.

Cole rubbed his forehead harder, wishing he could rub out the scripture verse that had flitted through his mind too many times since. He dropped his hand to the table and returned his focus to the deputy. "What are you doing to keep Sherri safe?"

"Sending a patrol car along on any calls. Not much more we can do."

That was something anyway. It would give him time to hang with Eddie without having to worry about Sherri every second. Helping Eddie escape the mess he'd made of his life was the whole reason he'd moved back to Stalwart. The attacks against Sherri had sidetracked him, but getting through to Eddie was no less urgent. Kids younger than him died of drug overdoses every day. And Eddie was clearly addicted.

The deputy grilled Cole about what he'd seen around the house before the explosion, which amounted to nothing helpful. The fire marshal had already confirmed it was a drug house, but they had yet to identify, let alone catch, the guy who'd escaped on the motorcycle.

"The house was a rental," the deputy explained. "And the name on the lease agreement turned out to be fake. Our working theory is that he'd already had the house rigged to blow to give himself a chance to get away if the need ever arose. It doesn't seem likely he could've done it in the short time you were there."

Cole studied the descriptions of the renter offered by neighbors. "Yeah, I'm not buying that he's the one targeting Sherri, either. Not when he had to know his operation would be outed by luring her to the house. I think we need to look for the guy who gave Eddie the tip."

"Sure." Skepticism flickered in the deputy's eyes. Apparently he wasn't buying that Eddie was being framed. "But your brother's description doesn't give us much to go on." The deputy closed the file. "The guy's heavier than the motorcyclist and balding. That probably describes half the men over thirty in town."

Yeah, and chances were the suspect wouldn't risk making contact with Eddie again anytime soon. But if Cole could convince Eddie to show him around his usual haunts they might find him that way.

As Cole stepped out of the police station a few minutes later, the urge to drop in on Sherri before seeing Eddie drew his gaze across the street. The fire station blocked his view of the ambulance base, so he meandered toward the street. After all, the least he owed Sherri and Dan were coffee and a donut to thank them for yanking him away from that drug house the night before last. He pressed the butt of his hand to his throbbing temple. Besides, the caffeine might help kill his headache.

A guy in faded jeans and a dark hoodie skulked along the side wall of the ambulance base, his hands bunched in his pockets.

Cole quickened his steps. *The guy who sideswiped Sherri's ambulance had worn a hoodie.* Cole's gaze fixed on the punk's pocketed hands. The uneasy feeling that they concealed a weapon tripped his pulse into overdrive.

Sherri stepped out the front door, calling "Double? Double?" over her shoulder, oblivious to the threat lurking around the corner.

"Watch out!" Raising his hand stop-sign style, Cole dodged traffic, narrowly escaping being hit by a horn-blaring car. He glanced at it only a moment, but when he turned back to the ambulance base, Sherri was gone.

So was the punk.

FOUR

Sherri braced her hand on the door as Dan careened the ambulance onto Park Street. "Dispatch said he was on the north side of the park." She glanced in the side mirror as a patrol car turned onto the street behind them, and wondered what Cole had been shouting about when the call blared over the loudspeakers and she'd had to dash back inside. Her mind flashed to the sight of him cupping his forehead as they'd blasted out of the ambulance bay. He should still be on bed rest.

Dan pulled to the curb next to the four-acre park in the center of town. "He's over there." Dan pointed to a homeless man ranting at a rose bush. He wore several layers of filthy shirts and pants that once might have been tan in color. "It's Harold again."

"Yay," Sherri said mockingly. He was one of their frequent flyers and it was always a toss-up as to which personality they'd be dealing with. To make matters worse, he was borderline diabetic and lately he'd been spending more time over the line than not. They unloaded their gurney from the back of the truck.

The deputies met them at the curb. "Maybe we should handle this."

Harold's gaze snapped their way and his entreaties to the rose bush grew louder. "Watch out. Hide. They're coming. They're coming."

Sherri felt sorry for the poor man. He wasn't enough of a threat to himself or others to warrant locking him up, but he refused to stay at the shelter, where staff could help him monitor his blood sugar and his meds, if he'd take them. "Let's see what we're dealing with first. He's usually harmless enough when he's only ranting at vegetation."

Dan wrinkled his nose. "At least the roses might mask his BO. Last time we transported him to the ER it took half a can of air freshener to kill the smell afterward."

At that reminder the deputies looked a little too happy to step back and let them take the lead.

A couple of blond-haired youngsters raced over to them from the playground and gaped up at the deputies in wide-eyed awe. "Are you going to arrest that man? He's scary."

Their mother caught up to them a moment later and caught their hands. "I'm sorry. I told them to stay on the playground. I'm the one that made the call. I've seen him here a lot, but never like this."

"Thank you, ma'am," Deputy Vail said. "We'll see to him. It'd be best if you take the children home now."

Sherri circled upwind of Harold so he'd see her approach and lifted her hands palms out to appear unthreatening. "Good morning, Harold. What's bothering you today?"

His nostrils flared. "I'm not going with you."

She patted the air. "That's okay, Harold. Let's just talk." His breathing appeared normal. He wasn't clutching his chest. His eyes seemed to focus on her okay, although they immediately darted back to the rosebush.

"Don't let her take you," he hissed to the bush. It would've been comical if he weren't dead serious.

"He doesn't seem disoriented," Dan said. "Or aggressive like the last time his blood sugar nosedived. We're likely not looking at a diabetic issue, and something tells me he's not going to willingly let us take a sample anyway."

"Harold, have you had anything to eat this morning?" She took a step closer. "Can we get you something? You guys have any extra donuts in the cruiser," she called over her shoulder to a grumbled chorus of "Ha-ha." Harold didn't seem to think the quip was funny, either.

In a blur of motion he pulled a knife from his

pocket—a dinner knife—but it was startling enough that the deputies closed in.

"Get her, officers," Harold ordered them. "She's an alien. She's trying to abduct me."

Deputy Vail motioned her back. "Okay, Harold. Take it easy." As Vail kept him distracted, the other deputy skirted behind him and easily commandeered the knife, then cuffed him.

Harold went berserk. "Not me. Not me." He jerked from side to side, trying to break out of the deputy's hold. "She's the one you have to stop."

"Take it easy, Harold. We'll make sure she doesn't get you." Deputy Vail winked at Sherri. "I guess *we'd* better deliver him to the ER."

The other deputy approached with Harold.

"Whoa." Vail stepped back and pinched his nostrils. "On second thought—"

"Nope." Dan started pushing the gurney back to the truck. "He's all yours."

The deputies escorted Harold to their cruiser, but when he spotted her helping Dan load the gurney on the truck, he went berserk.

"You won't get away with it. I know what you are. They told me. They told me."

Terrific. He was hearing the voices again. She should've figured. Across the street passersby stopped to stare at her. Cole pulled up in his pickup. What was he doing here?

"I'm going to get you," Harold vowed. "As soon as I get out, I'm going to kill you!"

The deputy shoved him into the back of the cruiser. "You don't want to do that."

Cole stalked across the street, fists clenched, expression fierce, looking ready to tear the poor man limb from limb.

My hero.

Deputy Vail intercepted him with a palm to his chest. "This isn't your man. He's a regular. Made the same threat to me four weeks ago, and today I'm his best friend. Why don't you follow the ambulance back to the base?"

Cole held his ground for another thirty seconds, his glare burning a hole through the cruiser's rear window, before he finally took a step back and let the deputy climb in his car.

"What are you doing here?" Sherri allowed herself a moment to relish the sight of him back on his feet. He wasn't in uniform, but that didn't diminish his commanding presence one iota. And only intensified her wholly inappropriate pleasure at seeing him here looking so protective of her. "You're supposed to be resting."

His surreptitious visual sweep of the surrounding park and streets before he joined her on the sidewalk chilled her a hundred times more than Harold's empty threats. "Who was that guy? Has he threatened you like that before?"

"He's harmless," Dan assured, slamming the ambulance's rear doors shut. "He has a psychotic episode every once in a while, but he doesn't have the power to back up his threats. And he doesn't remember them by the time he comes back to his senses."

Cole searched her eyes, clearly not ready to take Dan or the deputy's word for it.

Sherri shrugged. "What did you expect? This is an ordinary day in the life of a paramedic. Last week, I got a marriage proposal from a prisoner we transported."

Dan guffawed. "Oh, yeah. A real winner. Missing half his front teeth but sporting a six-pack."

Cole tensed. "Is he still in jail? How did he take your refusal?"

Sherri reached for the passenger door handle with a teasing grin. "What makes you think I refused?"

Cole pressed his fingertips to his forehead and temple. "Sherri, you're not taking this serious enough."

She squeezed his arm, secretly pleased by his concern even though it was his brother he should have been focusing on. "I'm fine. But you look like you should be in bed. Head injuries are nothing to mess with. Just because the MRI was clear doesn't mean you won't have any problems if you try to do too much too soon. What are you doing here anyway?"

"Making sure that guy didn't come after you."

"The homeless guy?"

"No, the guy in the hoodie I spotted skulking outside the ambulance base as you came out to get coffees."

Her heart hopscotched over a few beats, but she managed to keep her expression neutral. "That's why you shouted and pulled the kamikaze routine through traffic?"

His hands fisted again and he looked ready to blow a gasket. "He was seconds away from ambushing you. If that call hadn't come in when it did—" he glanced around again, scraping his hand across his forehead "—who knows what he might have tried. He must've run off when he heard me shout. I searched the area, but couldn't track him, so I followed you here to make sure he didn't show up."

"Cole, you shouldn't be out racing around after me." Oh, boy, not something she'd ever thought she'd hear herself say to Cole. But she couldn't him let him get any closer for both their sakes. His brother needed him. And she needed *not* to need him. His mile-wide, protective streak was entirely too attractive, and if she wasn't careful, she'd start admitting things he didn't need to know. She opened the side door of the ambulance and pressed him to sit on the step. Then flicked her penlight over his eyes, trying not to notice the intriguing shades of blue radiating from his shrinking pupils.

"I'm fine. I need to be out there finding that punk before he shows up on your doorstep."

She checked his blood pressure, her own spiking at the notion that some creep might show up at her apartment. "The deputies are following all our calls, and Dan is with me. I will be perfectly safe. You need to rest."

"I've rested enough," he said in a growl.

She lost her patience. "Then spend time with your brother. Considering where he turned up Friday night, he clearly needs help sooner rather than later."

The next afternoon Cole shifted in his truck seat, trying to get comfortable. He was still on sick leave, so he'd been parked in the coffee shop's back lot with a bird's eye view of the ambulance base since Sherri arrived for her shift this morning. She'd been right about him needing to spend time with his brother, and as much as her scolding had stung, Cole appreciated her concern. He'd kind of enjoyed her playing paramedic on him again, too—looking so intently at his eyes that he'd started to feel as if she could see into his very soul. He hadn't been able to get her deep blue eyes off his mind since. He just wished she exhibited half as much concern for herself.

Thankfully, the punk hadn't come back, and so far not even an ambulance call had come in to break up the monotony. He couldn't help but admire how easily she'd sloughed off the homeless guy's threat yesterday and joked about a prisoner's marriage proposal.

Yeah, it was how most frontline workers dealt with the junk, but she'd seemed genuinely unaffected.

Cole glanced at his watch. Eddie would be getting out of school in another forty-five minutes, and he didn't want to miss him again. Unfortunately, if the kid he'd spotted skulking around the ambulance base yesterday was also in school, he might show up just when Cole needed to leave.

Cole unscrewed his thermos cap and eyeballed the last few ounces of day-old coffee. *Forget it.* Time to grab a fresh cup. As he pushed open the door, movement along the fence behind the ambulance base caught his eye.

He soundlessly pushed his truck door closed and hunched down behind the hood.

A kid clambered over the chain-link fence. Same black hoodie hiding his face.

The instant he moved toward the ambulance base's side door, Cole dashed forward and faceplanted him into the dirt. Wrestling the guy's arm behind his back, he hissed, "What are you doing here?"

The punk stopped fighting. "Cole?"

Cole's stomach tanked. "Eddie?" He grabbed a fistful of his brother's hoodie and hauled him to his feet, scarcely restraining the urge to connect his fist with Eddie's nose. He clearly didn't know him anymore. "How could you?"

Eddie's eyes ballooned. "How could I what? I came to apologize to Sherri."

"Right." Cole felt sick. "That's why you're skulking over the fence, instead of walking up from the street."

"I didn't want the other guys to see me. I wanted to catch her alone."

Cole swallowed a rush of bile at how that sounded. He shoved his brother through the hedge flanking the parking lot toward the coffee shop next door. "We need to talk."

"I'm telling the truth!"

Cole opened the coffee shop door and motioned Eddie to a window seat.

"I always liked Sherri. She was nice to us."

A waitress sashayed over, clunked two empty mugs on the table, and flashed Cole a welcoming whatcha-doing-later smile. "You must be new here. I never forget a face." She had pouty lips and an over-the-top makeup job that he supposed some guys would find attractive.

"That's right." He pushed his cup toward the pot in her hand.

"What can I get you boys?" she asked as she filled both mugs.

"A couple of the specials," Cole ordered to expedite her exit.

"Two specials coming up." She winked and flounced away, leaving a trail of fragrance lingering behind her.

Eddie snagged the sugar dispenser and dosed his coffee with a steady stream. "Still a chick magnet, I see."

Cole popped a couple of ibuprofen to take the edge off the headache that had returned with a vengeance thanks to their scuffle, and tried to decide if he heard derision or jealousy in Eddie's tone. Probably a little of both. If Eddie spent half his time tripping out, Cole couldn't imagine too many girls being interested in hanging with him. At least no one who wasn't stoned herself.

Eddie stirred his coffee so hard it swirled over the brim. "C'mon, why don't you just get the lecture over so we can both go home?"

"You expect me to believe you came here to apologize to Sherri?"

"Yes."

"The guy who lured you to the drug house didn't send you here?"

"What? No!"

Cole exhaled, unfortunately believing him, which meant he was back to square one. "Okay, I'm sorry I doubted you. I'm afraid we didn't get off to a good start, but believe it or not, I came back to Stalwart because I want to spend time with you, not lecture you."

"Don't do me any favors. I got over my case of big brother worship a long time ago."

Yeah, Eddie hadn't appreciated Cole's opinion on his choice of who to live with after the divorce. Almost a year had passed before they'd even talked to each other again. "I'm sorry. I was wrong to stay away so long. I'm hoping we can make up for lost time."

Eddie snorted. "Face-planting me into the sidewalk is a great way to start." He lifted his mug in a toast. "Thanks."

The waitress slipped their soup bowls onto the table, allowing him to let the remark pass without comment. Clearly it would take a lot more than a few shared dinners to chisel that boulder-sized chip from Eddie's shoulder.

Sirens cut through the silence. An ambulance whipped out the bay next door, but with hedges blocking a good part of the view, Cole couldn't tell if Sherri was inside. He breathed a silent prayer for her protection that only partially quelled the urgent desire to follow the ambulance and do the job himself. Okay, time to stop worrying about treading on his brother's feelings. He locked gazes with Eddie. "If you want me to trust you, you need to be straight with me. 'Cause I'll tell you, across the street is an office full of deputies that think you should be sitting in jail. Are you stalking Sherri?"

"What?" Eddie's head jolted back, his eyes wide with shock that looked pretty believable, unless it was shock that Cole had clued into his double life. If Eddie was trying to exact revenge for the way Cole had ignored him, terrorizing Sherri was a sickeningly smart way to go.

"You heard me," Cole said through gritted teeth, not wanting to believe the worst about Eddie despite appearances.

"No, man, I just needed a fix." He raked his fingers through his hair. "I thought you of all people would believe me."

"I want to, Eddie. But you're not giving me anything to go on. You say some guy told you to do these things, but you don't have a name, a location and scarcely a description. And her partner's got it in for you now." Cole had checked the guy's background. A former army medic, the man had a little too much righteous warrior in him for Cole's comfort level.

"I'm telling you, that day in the ambulance is the first time I'd seen her in, like—" he hesitated, the flick of his gaze betraying his deception "—like, forever."

Cole let it slide. *For now.* If he wanted to earn Eddie's trust, he needed his brother to at least think he believed him. "And where were you when this *guy* told you to raid her ambulance?"

"Around."

"Around where?"

"I don't remember. The park maybe."

"The park downtown?" Where psycho homeless guy hung out.

"Yeah, maybe. I hang there sometimes. It's not like I go looking for him." Eddie slurped his soup. "He finds me."

Cole didn't like the sound of that. "He finds *you*?"

"Yeah, you know. We just kind of run into each other."

Yeah, Cole could imagine the kind of places they ran into each other. If anyone had asked him seven years ago if there was a booming drug culture in Stalwart, he would've laughed. Now…he wasn't so sure. "You hang out together?"

"No, but he knows what it's like to, you know, need a fix."

Needing to get his own fix on the guy's whereabouts, Cole resisted the urge to point out that the guys at Teen Challenge knew, too, and cared a whole lot more about helping him. Eddie wasn't ready to hear it yet.

"He sometimes gives me tips on where I can get stuff free," Eddie went on.

"You mean steal it?"

Eddie shrugged again.

"What's he drive?"

"Never paid attention."

"But he does drive? He's not some homeless guy living on the street?"

"He doesn't look like one." Eddie pushed away his empty soup bowl. "We done?"

Cole's cell phone buzzed. He glanced at the screen. Zeke? He'd thought his partner would be happy to have another day off from being saddled with him. Probably calling to rub in that his nephew wouldn't be taking a sick day if he were on the job. Cole held up a finger to signal Eddie to wait a minute and clicked Talk. "What's up?"

"You know where your brother is?" Zeke's voice grated. Why the sheriff had partnered Cole with the one guy who resented him filling the new opening, he'd never know.

"Here with me. Why?"

Eddie's wary gaze snapped to his.

"You're lucky. Dispatch just got a call of a savage dog attacking a female paramedic."

Cole's pulse jumped. Sherri was the only female paramedic in Stalwart. "Where? Is she okay?"

"I don't know what her condition is. I'm on my way. So's animal control. She's at Line One near Third."

"Thanks for letting me know."

Zeke's snort punctuated the click of him hanging up. Clearly his intention hadn't been friendly.

Cole threw cash on the table and grabbed Eddie's arm. "We've got to go." Zeke may have taken his word that Eddie was with him, but he wanted Sherri to see it for herself.

"Me?" Eddie looked as if he thought Cole was taking him to a lynching—his.

FIVE

"Nice dog," Sherri repeated to the snarling Rottweiler, her heart jack-hammering her ribs.

Dan, who'd gotten away by ramming the dog with the gurney, was frantically trying to get dispatch to raise their 9-1-1 caller. "I told you I had a bad feeling about this place."

"Now? You really want to have this argument now?" His battering-ram routine hadn't helped the situation. Eyes fixed on the hundred-pound mass of heaving muscle and bared teeth, she continued her slow back pedal. She already had one inquest hanging over her head. Making another patient wait because of a *feeling* hadn't been an option. One more backward step and the jagged stucco of the L-shaped house dug into her spine.

Her heart jumped to her throat. The dog had her cornered in the middle of the L, a good hundred feet from the safety of the ambulance. "What do I do now?" She breathed through clenched teeth.

"Try holding out your hand like you're friendly."

"Are you crazy? He'll bite it off."

"Okay." Abandoning his radio, Dan edged forward and cautiously reached for the overturned gurney.

Like lightning, the dog dug its teeth into the cushioned top and with a whip of its head sent the gurney clattering.

Sherri edged sideways along the wall as Dan sprang back and nearly went down.

But the dog didn't pounce on him. It immediately retrained its narrowed black eyes on her and stalked closer inch by menacing inch.

Reaching behind her, she felt for the doorknob. It didn't give.

Sweat trickled down her cheeks. Dan was yelling something, but she couldn't make out what over the roar of blood pulsing past her ears.

Finding the doorbell, she drilled it with her thumb. "Nice doggie," she repeated.

With a blood-chilling growl, the dog bared its fangs.

"Dan!"

"Yah, yah!" he yelled and jumped around like a crazy man. "Help is coming, Sherri. Just don't make any sudden moves." Except Dan's sudden moves weren't doing a thing to distract the beast.

She struggled to pull in a breath. They'd warned her about dogs in training. But she couldn't remember a thing they'd said. "Am I supposed to maintain eye contact?" She hadn't dared take her eyes off of him.

"Yeah, I think so," Dan said between "yahs."

She tried showing it an open palm like he'd suggested earlier.

"No, don't look him in the eye!" A guy rushed toward them, scooping up a dead branch as he ran. "Look at its ears or feet, or it'll think you're challenging him. And fist your hands. Pull them close to your body. Don't give him anything to bite."

She instantly shifted her gaze to its ears, gulped at their pointy tips aimed straight at her face.

"Go home!" the guy ordered. "Bad dog. Go home!"

"It's not listening," Sherri eked out. She chanced a glance back at its eyes and the dog lunged.

Massive paws slammed into her, driving the air from her chest. Razor-sharp teeth sliced through her shoulder.

"Cover your face!" The guy swung the branch toward them.

The dog snapped its head around and caught the limb in its teeth. She pushed at its chest, trying to get out from under him. Pain screamed through her shoulder. "Get him off me!"

* * *

"Stay in the truck," Cole ordered Eddie as they careened to a stop behind an orange car parked behind Sherri's ambulance. The sound of her scream ripped through his chest. Drawing his gun, he raced toward Dan and another guy waving their arms and bouncing around like rodeo clowns.

At the sight of Sherri pinned to the ground by a monstrous dog, its paws on her chest as it viciously tore into her, Cole's heart lurched. He skidded to a stop and got a bead on the dog. Sweat stung his eyes as his finger trembled over the trigger. Blocking out her screams, he inhaled, the scent of blood so strong he could taste it. *Aim center mass and shoot to stop the threat.* His field training officer's instructions blasted through his brain. But Sherri was under that mass!

He jerked up his arms and squeezed off a shot.

The bullet pinged the stucco wall, distracting the dog enough to break his bite, and Cole's heart kicked back to life.

The guy with the branch stormed in again, swinging.

The dog lunged for the tree limb as, gripped by the image of it mauling Sherri, Cole tried to get another bead on it.

Two animal control officers raced up. "It's okay. We got it."

The guy wrestling with the dog flung the branch at it and scaled the wall as effortlessly as Spider-Man would have.

The animal jumped and tried to clamber after him.

The guy clung to an awning with one hand, his feet and other hand braced against adjoining walls as the dog's heavy claws tore at the stucco. Its snapping jaw narrowly missed the guy's foot.

"We got it," one of the animal control officers repeated, angling around the dog with a long pole with a loop attached.

Holstering his gun, Cole raced to Sherri's side, his stomach clenching at the sight of the blood-drenched bandage Dan had pressed against her shoulder. "What can I do?"

"Grab the trauma bag!" Dan jutted his chin toward an overturned gurney.

Cole righted the gurney, unbelted the bag secured on top and skidded to his knees at Sherri's side.

Dan's gaze flashed to the dog that animal control was still struggling to subdue. "Help me get her to the ambulance."

She groaned and pushed onto her hands and knees. "I can get up." She staggered to her feet, her pallor grayer than the weathered stucco.

Cole scooped her into his arms—how perfectly she fit—and hurried toward the ambulance. "Grab the door," he shouted at Dan as her lips pinched into a white line. "It's okay. You're going to be okay. Hang on." He slowed a fraction to keep from jostling her and shot a glance over his shoulder to ensure the dog hadn't veered back in their direction.

The animal-control officers had it cornered, but the dog's ears suddenly perked.

Cole curled his arms to bring Sherri snug against his chest and ran the last five yards to the back of the ambulance, ignoring the pounding pain that stormed into his head at the exertion. Two steps ahead of him, Dan shoved the recovered gurney aboard then grabbed Cole by the top of his sleeve and hauled them up into the ambulance a second before the dog lunged their way.

"Lay her on the gurney," Dan ordered, but Cole couldn't make his arms cooperate.

She was trembling viciously against his chest and the thought of letting go seemed wrong on too many levels. What if this attack was deliberate? Could he trust Dan with her care?

The ambulance's side door burst open, and Eddie's face bobbed into view. "Cole, we have to go."

Dan swung toward the door. "You!" He brandished the scissors he'd been about to take to Sherri's shirt and looked at Cole's brother as if he'd tear him to pieces.

"Eddie didn't have anything to do with this," Cole said quickly. "We were at the coffee shop in town when the call came in."

The man's jaw worked back and forth, as if he wasn't ready to swallow the excuse.

But the uncertainty trembling in Sherri's eyes as she tried to push out of his arms bothered Cole more. He set her gently onto the gurney.

"We've got to go *now,*" Eddie pressed.

The back door burst open, and a paramedic whose name Cole couldn't remember jumped into the rig. "What have you got?"

"Dog bite in the shoulder." Dan tore off Sherri's sleeve, revealing raw, ragged flesh.

Eddie turned away and heaved.

Cole focused his attention on Sherri's face, swallowing hard.

"I'm fine." She rolled onto her uninjured side as if she intended to get up.

"Take it easy, superwoman." Dan pressed her back to the gurney as the other paramedic checked her vitals and muttered about irresponsible owners. "Is Bill checking on our 9-1-1 caller?"

"Yeah, but sounds like it might've been another crank call. Neighbor says the homeowner's been in the hospital for weeks."

Cole wouldn't have thought it possible, but Sherri's face turned even grayer.

"Cole." His brother's impatient bark hit him like a blow to the back.

He spun on his heel. "What?"

"The woods. We have to check them out. Didn't you see the way the dog's ears perked? Someone blew a whistle."

What Eddie had been trying to tell him finally sank in. Someone had called the dog off. And that someone had to be in the woods the dog had lurched toward!

Cole's gaze snapped to Dan.

"I'll take care of her," he said, already dousing the wound with saline. "Find the creep who did this."

"Right." Cole barreled out the door. "C'mon, Eddie." They sprinted to the two animal control officers who were lifting the tranquilized Rottweiler into a cage on the back of their truck. "You see whoever was blowing that whistle?"

"Saw movement in the woods over there." The officer jutted his chin toward the woods across the street. "Didn't get a good look, though."

"Okay, thanks." Cole glanced back at the yard where Zeke was still questioning neighbors, then motioned to Eddie. "C'mon." They raced into the woods, but picking up the trail in the rotted leaves matting the ground proved difficult.

"Over there!" Eddie pointed to a muddy boot print on a rock, then another a yard away.

"He was probably heading toward Third Street." Dodging tree branches, Cole raced that direction. Chances were that if the guy didn't live nearby, he'd have a car parked on Third. The smell of rotting leaves and damp earth clawed at his throat. If this guy got to his car before Cole caught up to him— Cole cut off the thought and ran harder.

Brighter light filtered through the trees. The road had to be close.

An engine roared to life.

Cole sprinted toward the sound, broke past the tree line. But the road was deserted. He slammed his palm into a tree trunk. "We lost him." He fisted his hands against the sting of failure more than the sting in his palm. How many times would he let Sherri down?

Eddie hunched over, braced his hands on his knees and gulped air. "Can't you put out a BOLO?"

"For what? We don't even know what he's driving." And there weren't any houses around. Cole stalked back through the woods in the direction they'd come. "Our best hope of tracking him is if he had a dog license for that menace. He'll be looking at an attempted murder charge after I get through with the DA."

Eddie tripped over a tree root and his knees hit the dirt.

Extending a hand to help him up, Cole spotted a cell phone in the leaves. Using a tissue to preserve fingerprints, he picked it up. "You drop this?"

"No, I lost my phone a few days ago."

That explained, at least, why he hadn't responded to any of Cole's messages.

Eddie wiped his dirt-smeared hands down his jeans. "You think it's the guy's we were chasing?"

"If it's still got juice, chances are good it is." Cole hit the power button and the screen lit. He grinned. "We've got him." Using a pen tip, he pushed a couple of buttons to pull up the contacts menu. "If we can't get an ID on the owner from the phone's number, we'll get it from his contacts." His heart jerked at the sight of an all-too-familiar phone number—his father and Eddie's home number.

Eddie's face turned as pale as Sherri's had been.

"Who's phone is this?" Cole demanded.

"I…I…" Eddie backed away looking guilty. *Very* guilty.

Cole fisted Eddie's shirt in his hand and backed him against a tree. "Who's terrorizing Sherri?"

"I don't know."

"Whose phone is this?" Cole demanded more loudly.

Eddie's mouth opened and closed, but nothing came out.

Cole shoved him hard against the tree. "Tell me."

"It's mine. It's my phone."

"Yours?" Cole's grip went lax. Eddie had been with him the whole time. There was no way he could've sicced that dog on Sherri, and if he knew who had, he wouldn't have pressed Cole to follow the dog. *Would he?*

"Can I have it back?" Eddie's voice quivered.

"No, we need to dust it for fingerprints." Cole's breath bottled up in his lungs. They'd find Eddie's prints, identify the phone as Eddie's, and take one look at his rap sheet and not believe for a second that he wasn't connected.

Alibi or not.

And Cole—the new cop brother—trying to defend him would *not* go over well.

Eddie tugged on his arm. "Cole, you can't turn it in. They'll think I'm trying to hurt her. You know they will. But I'm not. I swear I'm not."

Cole flung off his grasp, plodded back toward the road. "I can't withhold evidence." He could still picture the censure in Sherri's eyes when he'd begged her not to say anything about the pills she'd found in his pocket. "If this phone is found out later, it'll only make you look more guilty, like I was trying to cover for you."

"They wouldn't find out. 'Cause I'm not going to tell them. They'll put me in juvie this time for sure if you turn it in. Please, you can't do this to me. I'm your brother."

His conscience twinged. "I'm not doing it *to* you. I'm trying to stop whoever is terrorizing Sherri."

"So you're choosing her over me? Just like you always chose everyone else over me."

"What? That's not true." Except even as he said it the many times Eddie had begged him to play with him paraded through Cole's mind, and every time he'd chosen to go out with his buddies instead.

"You're just like Dad. You look like him. You sound like him. And you think like him. Family doesn't mean anything to you."

Cole rammed Eddie against a tree, rage boiling in his chest. "I'm nothing like that man." All his life he'd been told how much he was like his father. Until seven years ago it had seemed like a compliment. Now it ate at his insides like acid. "I'm here because of you. I left the Seattle police force and took this job because of you. Because I care about *you*."

Eddie shoved him away. "You got a funny way of showing it. And if you cared so much, why'd it take you seven years to come back? Huh?"

"Because you're not the only one Dad's choices hurt. Mom needed me. And I didn't trust myself not to rip him to pieces if I saw him again.

The only reason he sweet-talked you into staying was to spite her, and you were too thick-headed to see it."

The tears that sprang to Eddie's eyes hit Cole square in the gut. "I'm sorry. I didn't mean that."

"Yes, you did." Eddie stalked out of the woods.

Eddie had always been desperate for Dad's attention, because Dad had always favored Cole. Was it any wonder that Eddie had clung to the chance to be on the receiving end of the attention he'd always craved, no matter how dysfunctional Dad's motives? Clearly the attention hadn't lasted long.

Or were the drugs a desperate attempt to get it back?

Cole trailed Eddie out of the woods, kicking himself for blowing it so badly. It was almost a relief when Eddie started walking down the road instead of heading to Cole's truck. They both needed time to cool down.

The ambulance had left. Only Zeke and the wall-climbing guy were still at the scene. The guy shook Zeke's hand, then climbed in the orange car. At the sound of the engine roaring to life, Eddie turned and stuck out his thumb. The guy pulled up beside him, and Eddie climbed in.

Cole hovered on the opposite side of the road, his brother's phone heavy in his pocket. "So who was that guy?"

"Ted Holmes. He said he was driving by and saw the paramedics in trouble, so stopped to help." Zeke squinted from the disappearing car to Cole. "What happened with your brother?"

"We had a disagreement." Reaching for Eddie's phone, Cole crossed the road to hand it over to Zeke. Whatever evidence they could get off the phone might be the key to finding out who was terrorizing Sherri. No matter what Eddie thought about his loyalties, he owed Sherri that much.

SIX

Blood seeped through Sherri's fingers as she frantically piled more bandages on the wound, more and more bandages. But the bleeding wouldn't stop. The pop, pop, pop of gunfire wouldn't stop. The dog lunging at her wouldn't—

"Shh, it's okay. You're safe now," a tender voice whispered through the ones in her head. A warm hand squeezed her arm, compelled it to still.

She relaxed. Slowly turned her palm up. Her skin tingled at the rasp of fingers traveling down the tender inside of her arm, then closing possessively around hers.

Her heart jolted. Where was she? She clawed out of her dream's residual emotions and opened her eyes.

Cole smiled down at her—an uncertain smile that didn't touch his eyes. "Hey," he said, his voice hoarse. "Bad dream?"

She blinked, reached up to scrub her eyes, certain she must still be dreaming. But the burning tug of her shoulder stitches grounded her firmly in reality. She discreetly pulled her sheets higher. Where was the nurse? She should've been back by now with the antibiotic shot so Sherri could get out of here.

Bad dreams she could handle. Cole she couldn't. Not here. Not now. Not when he looked at her as if she were as fragile as spun glass.

"Who's Luke?" he asked softly.

"What?" How did he know about—?

Heat climbed to her cheeks. *The nightmare.* She looked down the long room of curtained beds, anywhere but at Cole. The ER buzzed with its usual flurry of activity—the clatter of instruments, the beep of monitors, the hum of voices—sounds that usually eased her tension when bringing in a patient. Today the noise left her nerves frayed.

Where was Dan? Hadn't he said he'd only be a few minutes when he left to find her a shirt to wear home?

Cole had changed out of his bloodstained T-shirt into the kind of soft flannel shirt she used to imagine snuggling against on a cool evening. She still could feel how securely he'd held her earlier. So close she could hear his heart pound beneath her ear. He hadn't seemed to want to let her go, either, despite her accusation the night before last that he was enabling Eddie instead of helping him. Worse than that, she hadn't wanted him to let her go.

Oh, this was so not good. Ignoring his question about Luke, she strained for a light tone. "Don't tell me my partner wrangled you into driving me home?"

"No, but I'd be happy to." He grinned as though he meant it.

Her fingers tightened around the bedsheets. "Thanks, but that's okay." Cole might not be wearing his uniform, but she could see the questions in his eyes. And could imagine what he might've overheard her babbling in her sleep. "Dan'll be here any minute." She couldn't believe she'd actually dozed off. "Um…" She squinted up at him. "Why are you here?"

His eyebrow arched as if he thought she was as addled as she felt with the painkillers fogging her brain. "I'm trying to figure out who sicced that dog on you. Did you recognize the dog? Was it Luke's?"

"No! Why would you think that?"

His head tilted, his scrutiny intensifying. "You were wrestling the dog in your sleep and muttered the name Luke more than once."

The blood drained from her face, and a numbing chill iced her veins. "It was just a dream." Except…the memory of Luke's father confronting her after the interment flared in her mind. Luke's devoted dog had been there, too. She squinted, trying to picture what breed it had been, but could only recall how pitifully it had whined as the casket had been lowered into the ground.

"Are you sure?" Cole grilled, yanking the privacy curtain farther around the bed.

"Yes, I'm sure."

"Because I pulled the dog license records for Stalwart and the surrounding county. A Luke Atkins was the first name on the list, and he owns a Rottweiler."

Yes, his dog had been a Rottweiler. She remembered now. The poor thing had refused to budge from its place next to Luke's open grave, and she'd knelt down to stroke its head.

Luke's father had gone berserk, yanked her away, told her she'd had some nerve showing up at his boy's funeral. He'd told her Luke would still be alive if she'd done her job.

Steeling herself against the crushing weight of *that* reminder, she buzzed the nurse. If they'd get here with the antibiotic shot already, she could go.

Cole's fingers skimmed her jaw, gently turning her face to his. "What's wrong? Can I help?"

"I was just wondering what the holdup was on my needle." Sherri avoided his gaze. All this time she'd been so sure it had been her crew driving her to quit she hadn't even thought of Luke's father.

Cole's hand fell away from her face. "Sherri,

I can't help you if you don't tell me what's going on. Who's Luke?"

The image of Luke's blood seeping through her fingers seared her mind. She sucked in deep breaths, her hands pressing into her chest as if pushing harder would stop the bleeding. *Oh, God, please don't let me fall apart here. Please.* She buried her hands under her armpits and willed her emotions into submission.

"Who? Is? Luke?" Cole demanded. "Do you think he's behind these attacks?"

She choked on the lunacy of the notion. "No, of course not."

Cole's gaze darkened. "How do you know?"

Fighting back tears, she clasped her hand over her mouth and shook her head.

"How do you know?" he repeated more insistently.

"Because he's dead." Dan stepped around the curtain and shot Cole a look so heated it would have melted steel.

A guttural moan escaped Cole's throat, his hold slackening. "I'm sorry."

Her heart stuttered at the empathy in his tone, at his stricken look. "He was my partner," she whispered. "He died five months ago."

Before Cole could plug her for details, Dan, bless his heart, thrust a small bouquet into her hands. "From the guys."

The bundle of mums, freesias and carnations was the kind that sat in water buckets at the grocery checkout—colorful but already a little droopy.

"Thank them for me." Sherri blinked back tears, knowing she shouldn't be touched. It was standard policy to chip in for something whenever anyone on the team got injured. Except maybe she'd misjudged them. Maybe Luke's father had been behind everything. If anyone hated her enough to hurt her, it would be him. Or maybe no one was and she was just being paranoid.

No, not paranoid. Just because some stupid online test said she had post-traumatic stress disorder didn't make it so. Dan was the one who'd insisted Cole investigate, not her. Sure, she'd been a little jumpy since Luke's death, and yeah, she'd had nightmares. Who wouldn't?

But she was *not* paranoid.

"You got a lead on who did this?" Dan snapped at Cole, his eyes narrowing. "Besides your brother."

"Not yet." The twitch in Cole's cheek betrayed the sting of Dan's accusation. Or maybe he was thinking of her initial suspicions that put Dan and his buddies at the top of the suspect list. Cole unfolded a piece of paper and held it in front of her. "These are the names of every licensed Rottweiler owner in the county. Do you recognize any of the names besides Luke's?"

Dan snorted. "Do you really think a guy who'd sic a ferocious dog on someone is going to bother buying a dog license?"

"At this point this is all we have to go on. No one in the vicinity recalled seeing a vehicle parked on the other side of the woods or anyone out walking a Rottweiler."

Sherri set the flowers on her lap and took the paper from him. "What are the Xs beside the names for?"

"Those are dogs that have been microchipped. The dog we captured hasn't been. So we eliminated those owners as likely suspects, although we will pay each and every one a visit, as they may own more than one dog despite only paying to license one."

As she scanned the list, her heart grew heavier. "I don't recognize any of the names."

"What about the addresses?"

Confused, she squinted up at him. "How does that help?"

Dan caught a corner of the paper and tilted it his way. "Could be someone we treated…only not to their satisfaction."

"Reinhart?" Sherri gasped, scanning the list for his apartment address, except he never had a dog.

"He's not on the list," Cole said, clearly having formulated the same theory as Dan. "I also cross-referenced his son's address. No match."

Dan studied the list with an intensity that surprised her.

"Do you recognize any of the names or addresses? We could compare them to our call records."

"No, I don't." Dan shook his head, but continued to study the list.

Sherri curled and uncurled the edge of her blanket, feeling antsier by the second. "Maybe this nut job just has it in for paramedics in general. He had no way of knowing whether we or the other team would respond to the call. Or that the dog would target me rather than Dan, for that matter." That realization minutely eased the knot in her stomach.

"It's possible," Cole said, not sounding as if he thought so. He reclaimed the list and pulled out a notepad and pen. "I need you to tell me anything that might offer us a clue to this guy's identity or motive." Cole's gaze took in both her and Dan. "No matter how unlikely it seems."

She edged toward the head of the bed. There was no way she'd add insult to injury by speculating that Luke's father might be out for revenge. She'd hurt the man enough. If, once she got out of here, she found evidence he might be the culprit, then she'd tell Cole. Or better yet, her sher-iff-deputy-cousin Sam, if he ever got back from his honeymoon.

Dan's lips pressed flat. "I didn't like how the situation looked the second we pulled up. The lawn hadn't been mowed in weeks. Flyers were bleeding out of the mailbox."

"It was supposed to be a heart attack victim. Guys with heart trouble don't prioritize lawn care," Sherri argued. "But there wasn't supposed to be a dog. Dispatch always asks. The caller said no dog."

"The call was bogus!" Dan bounced his fin-gers off his forehead as if she were dense. "I'm telling you that somebody's targeting you. And he needs to be stopped before it's too late. That dog almost killed you today."

"You don't think I know that?" she roared back, not sure why she was arguing. "But the 9-1-1 caller couldn't know I'd respond to the call."

"He does if he's monitoring the radio and knows one ambulance is already out," Dan said, low and ominous, as if he wanted her more freaked than she already was.

"The question is why?" Cole cut in.

"How in blazes are we supposed to know that?" Dan wound his arms over his chest. "Maybe you should be asking that brother of yours."

Feeling Cole's wince, Sherri said, "Cut him

some slack." Dan knew Eddie had been with Cole when the call came in, but he was apparently still bent on goading him. Or…was he goading Cole to shift suspicions from him and his buddies?

After all, he'd been the one who'd told her to look the dog in the eye and to hold out her hands to it, and…and…the dog had totally ignored him, even with all his "yahs" and wild gesticulating.

Listen to me. I really am paranoid.

"Cut him slack?" Dan's voice pitched so high the ER momentarily went quiet. Fisting his hands, he repeated in a hiss, "That. Dog. Almost. Killed. You." He turned back to Cole. "There's no good reason why anyone would hurt her. She's a nice person and a fine paramedic."

Sherri practically choked over the surprising claim. If only it were true, Luke's father wouldn't have had to bury his only son.

Cole nodded as if he couldn't agree more. "Do you know Ted?"

"Ted?" she and Dan asked at the same time.

"The guy who climbed the wall."

"Oh." Dan's posture relaxed, his arms dropping to his sides. "He told me he was driving by and heard her scream and stopped to help. I've never seen him before. The guy had guts, that's for sure." Dan snorted. "Or no brains. I've never seen anyone climb a wall like that. If he hadn't come along, I don't know what…" Dan's voice petered out as if the thought of her being critically hurt had swiped his breath.

Cole's fingers brushed over her blanket-covered leg, the intensity in his gaze suggesting he felt the same as Dan.

Her heart hiccupped.

"Is there someplace you can stay for a few days?" Cole held her gaze. "Until we catch this guy, I'd rest easier if you weren't staying on your own."

"She'll stay with us, of course." Mom swept aside the curtain tugged around the bed and she, Dad and her favorite cousin, Jake, still wearing his firefighter's uniform, poured into the tiny space. "How's our girl?"

"Who told you I was here?"

"Jake," Mom said with a hint of censure as she fussed with the blankets. "Why didn't you call us?"

Cole edged toward a break in the curtain panels, looking at her parents and Jake as if they were a firing squad.

The smidgen of relief she felt that he seemed as eager to avoid being recognized, as she was for Mom *not* to remember the huge crush her little girl had had on him, evaporated the instant Jake slapped Cole's shoulder and held on in a friendly grip. "Cole? Hey, good to see you. I didn't know you were back in town."

"He's our newest deputy sheriff," Sherri rushed to explain before Jake got the wrong idea about what Cole was doing at her bedside.

A big mistake. Mom and Dad had been peppering her with questions about what happened and why she never called. But the moment their attention swiveled to Cole, she could tell by Mom's elated smile that she thought she was looking at the answer. As for Dad…

Well, he didn't look too happy.

Seven-thirty Monday morning Cole drove to Sherri's parents' home to update her on the investigation. He wished he had better news. The streets were already humming with dog walkers, residents collecting their morning papers and young parents loading up kids to drop at daycare before their morning commute. He hoped the Steele household would be up, too, with a pot of coffee brewing.

He rubbed the dull throb at his temples. Forgoing a pain pill for his head this morning might've been a mistake. His doctor had warned him the concussion could get worse before it got better and had advised him to take off a couple more days, but with the investigation into the attacks on Sherri rapidly growing cold, that wasn't a prescription he was willing to stomach. He needed to convince Sherri to open up more. To trust him.

She was holding something back. He'd sensed it when he first interviewed her at the ambulance base. It had been obvious at the hospital. Not that he blamed her for clamming up about Luke. But he had an uneasy feeling that there'd been more to her silence than just grief.

Like something that could point him to who was really targeting her.

Somehow he needed to convince her to trust him with every suspicion, no matter how remote.

Last night Zeke reported he'd visited all the Rottweiler owners on the list—a mixed group ranging from geeky businessmen, who, according to Zeke, were probably hoping a Rottweiler would butch up their image, to brawny construction workers who could double as motorcycle gang members. Their wives, too, from their tattooed-to-the-hilt descriptions. Cole got the impression Zeke could've found a few things to arrest more than one of the owners for, but they'd all had a Rottweiler at home to alibi out of the attack on Sherri.

Which had left Sherri's dead partner's dog as the only suspect.

Cole winced, recalling her shattered look when he'd asked her if the dog had been Luke's. But *oh, man*, that look had been easier to take than her cringe when her mother had eagerly greeted him with a matchmaker's glint in her eye.

He'd been pleasantly stunned by how pleased her mom had been to see him, but by the sour note of her father's, "You're Al's boy?" he clearly didn't share his wife's enthusiasm for an alliance between him and Sherri.

Not that Cole blamed him. What father would want his only daughter attached to the son of a guy who'd pretend to be an upstanding believer on Sunday mornings and cheat on his wife the rest of the week? Let alone to the brother of a druggie.

Shaking off the thought, he turned into their subdivision. It wasn't as if he was vying for a relationship anyway. Except, given how quickly her family had changed the subject, he clearly hadn't put on a stellar performance of appearing unaffected by their reactions. He guessed he'd missed having a whole family more than he'd realized.

At least Sherri had a family who'd look out for her now that they knew how serious the situation was.

Cole took the long way to their house to take another pass by Luke's father's place three blocks east of it. A quick internet search had caught Cole up on the particulars of Luke's tragic death. And after Zeke's investigation had turned up nil, Cole had paid the old man a visit. But the Rottweiler lying in the backyard had squashed his theory that the grieving father was taking out his anger on his son's surviving partner.

Slowing his truck as he passed the shabby house, Cole slanted a glance down the side yard toward what was visible of the backyard's fence.

The sway of honey-blonde hair caught his attention.

He slammed his truck into Reverse and glanced down the shadowy narrow strip between the house and a six-foot hedge. *Sherri?* What on earth was she doing here?

His heart dropped. She must've suspected Luke's father, too. And hadn't trusted him enough to confide in him.

Cole pulled to the curb as barking erupted from the backyard. He jumped from his truck and charged in the direction he'd last seen her, pounding out his irritation that she'd come here alone.

Suddenly registering that the barking was a high-pitched yap, not the deep bass of the Rottweiler that had occupied the yard the day before, Cole skidded to a stop. Had the old man duped him? Anticipated they'd check on licensed owners and rustled up an imposter?

The hedge swished, and he spotted Sherri at the corner of the five-foot chain-link fence, shrouded by overgrown boughs. She threw a piece of meat into the yard and the yappy white terrier finally shut up. But from the angle of Sherri's head tilt, she was only interested in the mammoth doghouse by the back door. The doghouse where Luke's Rottweiler—at least the canine Cole had assumed was Luke's—had been contentedly sleeping the evening before.

Cole stole up behind her, trying not to notice how beautiful she looked in her billowy white blouse. "What's so interesting?" he whispered in her ear. The delicate fragrance of her hair caught him off guard, almost as off guard as he'd caught her.

She yelped and spun around on her heel, palm to her chest. "Cole, what are you doing here?"

Head pounding from his dash up the side yard, he lost his cool. "If you suspected Luke's father of siccing his dog on you, why didn't you tell me?"

"What? No, I didn't!"

"No? Then why are you sneaking up to his backyard to spy on—?"

The back screen door slammed open, and her panicked gasp sliced off the last of his question.

"He can't see me here." She bolted through the hedge and skirted along it on the neighbor's side.

"Sherri, wait," he hissed.

Her former partner's sour-faced father stalked across the backyard with a pronounced limp, his cane in one hand. The notion that he'd housed a Rottweiler impersonator to fool investigators last night had been ludicrous. There was no way he'd have been able to outrun Eddie and him in the woods yesterday.

The man glared at him through the fence. "What are you doing on my property—" his gaze traveled down Cole's uniform and back to his face "—deputy?"

"Yes, I'm Deputy Cole Donovan. We spoke last night. Remember?"

"Of course I remember. I'm not addled. What are you doing skulking around my property?"

"I apologize. I heard the dog barking and—"

"What do you want?" His arthritic hand fisted on the top of his cane.

"I was wondering where your son's Rottweiler is this morning." Cole paused, watching for a nervous twitch that might give away this man's involvement after all. Yesterday, he'd said the dog never went in the house. Yet, the doghouse was empty and the yappy terrier was the only canine in the yard. "Does someone walk him for you?"

Atkins flexed the fingers bunched over his cane. "What are you really asking?"

Cole stiffened at his defensiveness. "I'm asking where your dog is, sir."

Atkins scrutinized his yard's perimeter and then jutted his chin toward a freshly dug trench in the back corner. "He dug his way out again." His scowl darkened. "Check the cemetery. My son's grave is five rows from the back under the oak tree. That's where the dog goes when he gets out."

Cole nodded, his empathy for the man's pain warring with his fear the man would do anything to make Sherri pay for it. "Thank you. Sorry to have bothered you." Cole strode back alongside the stucco house toward the street and almost bowled Sherri over as she stepped around the hedge. She was clearly shaken from what she'd overheard.

"I'm so ashamed of myself for ever suspecting him. See, that's why I couldn't tell you. I've already hurt him enough."

Cole gripped her shoulders and tilted his head until she finally met his gaze. "Luke's death wasn't your fault," he said firmly. Except Atkins blamed her even though the man who'd squeezed the trigger—their patient's husband—was behind bars. Atkins had made that abundantly clear last night.

And Rottweiler accounted for or not, Atkins's attitude worried him.

Cole guided her toward his truck. "C'mon, I'll give you a ride back to your folks' place and fill you in on the investigation. You shouldn't be out walking alone these days."

She rammed her fisted hands into her hips. "I'm not going to let this creep beat me by cowering inside day and night. There are lots of people about this time of day. I don't think—"

"A dog could run out of anywhere and attack you?" Cole bit out. At her flinch and panicked glances to neighboring yards, he immediately closed his eyes and murmured an apology. Scaring her was not the way to win her trust. "I'm sorry. I don't want to see you hurt again."

Her expression softened as he opened the truck door for her. "I do appreciate your help."

His heart twisted at the vulnerability in her eyes, seriously messing with the professional distance he needed to keep. He strode around the hood, focusing instead on how to use her vulnerability to help him help her. Maybe he needed to do more than update her on the investigation. Maybe he needed to let her accompany him, since she was clearly going to investigate anyway. She'd be safer with him than out on her own. He could even take that extra day or two off work the doctor had suggested and investigate with her on his own time. He started the truck and turned toward the cemetery.

"I thought you were taking me home."

"Let's stop by the cemetery first and verify Atkins's story."

She nodded, averting her gaze back to the road, her throat working a visibly nervous rhythm.

He gritted his teeth against the ache building in his chest. Until a few days ago he'd managed to banish Sherri—the girl who'd bandaged his bruised heart along with his hand—from his thoughts most of the time. Now he couldn't get Sherri—the amazing woman she'd grown into—out of his head.

Or the uncoplike urge to mete out his own justice on her stalker.

SEVEN

Sherri couldn't stop the sob that burbled up her throat at the sight of Luke's beloved dog lying on his grave. Terrified of becoming completely unglued in front of Cole, she stumbled out of the truck and blindly hurried toward the grave. The dog shifted sad eyes toward her without raising his head, and let out a soulful whimper. She dropped to her knees at his side and buried her face in the fur at the back of his neck. "I miss him, too, boy. I'm so sorry. So very, very sorry."

The dog twisted his head and licked the tears streaming down her face. She forced a smile. "He loved you. He didn't want to leave you. You know that, don't you?" Lifting her gaze, she reached out and traced the letters of Luke's name etched in cold stone as the dog whimpered once more.

Cole coaxed her up from the damp ground and, unable to stop herself, she turned into his arms.

"He was a good man," she blubbered into his shirt. "Always helping people."

Cole rubbed her back. "Tell me about him."

She palmed tears from her face. "I'm sorry. I don't usually cry."

"There's nothing wrong with crying for someone you cared about."

"I wouldn't be a paramedic anymore if it weren't for Luke."

"How's that?"

She ducked her head, not really wanting to remember.

Cole recaptured her gaze, silently urging her.

Letting out a heavy sigh, she said, "We had a call to a little girl trapped in the back of a car. As firefighters worked to free her legs, I crawled in beside her under a blanket and sang songs to her and told her it was going to be all right. But she was in really rough shape, so when she asked about her mommy, I couldn't stop myself from telling her that her mommy was waiting for her, even though she'd died on impact."

Sherri choked up, the sound of the firefighter's power tools echoing through her mind. "A few seconds later, the little girl shouted, 'I see her. I see Mommy.' We were still under the blanket. She couldn't see anything and I felt horrible for giving her false hope."

Cole murmured something, but all she could hear was the phantom whir of a power saw.

"The next moment the little girl was gone, too."

Cole's arms tightened around her. "You made those final moments happy for her, instead of terrifying."

"That's what Luke said when I told him the next day I was quitting. That I couldn't handle watching another child die. He told me I'd made a difference. That I had a gift, and God wouldn't want me to throw it away. No one had ever told me that before. He made me promise I wouldn't quit."

"It sounds like he was a special man."

"Yes," she whispered. "His death was so senseless."

Cole smoothed her hair. "I don't pretend to know God's reasons, but I do believe that somehow He can bring good out of the tragedy."

She nodded, bumping her forehead against his chin. "I do believe that." She swiped at the last of her blasted tears. "I do." It was why she kept getting up every morning and not quitting. She had to believe that God had let her live for a reason. That he wanted her out there helping people.

Cole cradled her face in his palms and brushed the dampness from her cheeks with the pads of his thumbs. "You okay?"

She squirmed at the empathy in his voice. "Yes, thank you." And surprisingly, it was the truth. He'd witnessed her grieving the loss of a friend. That's all. Nothing worrisome about that. Nothing that would raise red flags about her fitness to return to work. Self-consciously she patted his damp shirt. Grief was natural. He'd said so himself.

He even sounded as if he might understand why she was so desperate to work every shift she could get. His thumb grazed her bottom lip and her gaze shifted to his lips, her heart galloping. Did he feel more than—?

"Sherri?" a high-pitched voice squealed. "Is this the young man your mother was telling me about?"

Cole's hands dropped to his sides, amusement dancing in his eyes. But he must've noticed her mortification, because he instantly sobered and turned to the elderly woman, hand extended. "Good morning, I'm Deputy Cole Donovan. I'm investigating the dog attack on Sherri."

"Oh." Mrs. Spiece shook his hand, her gaze bouncing from Luke's dog to Sherri's cheeks, which had to be flaming if the giddy smile that returned to Mrs. Spiece's lips was anything to go by. "Of course you are."

Sherri cringed at her lilt. Mrs. Spiece was the sweetest woman, but she was also the biggest storyteller in town.

"Nice to meet you. I must run. Tootle-loo." The woman waggled her fingers and headed back to her car, still carrying the flowers she'd arrived with.

"I'm sorry," Sherri blurted. "I'm afraid your innocent consoling hug will take on a life of its own by lunchtime."

He chuckled. "As long as they don't send a lynching party after me, no harm done."

"Are you kidding me? My mom adores you. But—" she tugged her bottom lip uncertainly between her teeth "—your girlfriend might not if she catches wind of their tall tales."

The grin that lit Cole's eyes said she hadn't fooled him by slipping in that little aside. He clearly knew she was fishing, and actually seemed flattered. "No girlfriend." The slam of a car door yanked their attention to the driveway. "Uh-oh."

Sherri's stomach bottomed out. *Luke's father.*

The sun disappeared behind a cloud as Mr. Atkins drilled Cole with a caustic glare. "What are you doing bringing *her* here?"

"She misses your son, too, sir."

He stalked toward them, glaring at her. "It should've been you."

Her knees buckled.

Cole's arm clamped securely around her waist, but he couldn't shield her from the image streaming across her brain. A vision of Luke's blood seeping over her hands.

Luke's father snapped a lead on the dog's collar and tugged him toward the car.

Cole curled his fist, looking as if he wanted to hurt the man. "He's wrong."

Her breaths were coming too fast and shallow. She forced herself to breathe slow and deep, already regretting how far she'd let Cole inside her head. "He's grieving," she rationalized, almost managing to sound unaffected by the man's appearance.

"That's no excuse."

Cole's palm came to rest comfortingly at the small of her back. "For the record, Atkins is still on my suspect list. He may not have pulled any of the stunts against you, but he could have masterminded them."

Sherri drew in a fortifying breath. If they were going to work together to figure out what was really going on, she needed to tell him everything. "You should know that my colleagues blame me for Luke's death, too. Not as overtly as Mr. Atkins. But I hear them whispering. That's the real reason I've always figured they were behind the pranks. To goad me into quitting. And that's why I was determined not to let the incidents ruffle me. I promised Luke I wouldn't quit."

"We're way past pranks, Sherri. And trust me, your colleagues are on my radar." He prodded her toward his truck.

"So what do we do now?"

"We pull in every piece of data we can get our hands on. We'll cross-reference the date and time of each incident with the schedules of every potential person who could've helped orchestrate them, starting with your colleagues, 9-1-1 operators and dispatch. And every person you can think of who could have the slightest motive—ex-boyfriends, wannabe boyfriends, patients or family members of patients who didn't like your treatment."

"I already told you—"

He cut her off with a wave of his hand and motioned for her to climb in. "You'll be surprised how many names we can come up with after we're through brainstorming."

Her gaze snapped to rustling in the bushes on the far side of the cemetery. Across the street, a man sat behind the wheel of an idling car.

This was crazy. Cole was making her paranoid.

"We need to look at anyone you might've crossed some time before the incidents started, from the guy you cut off on your way to work to the fellow tenant whose parking spot you usurped."

"What?" Her attention snapped back to Cole. "I never took anyone's parking spot."

"It was just an example. Nutcases have killed for less."

"Killed?" The word came out scarcely above a

whisper. She suddenly felt lightheaded. Sure, that drug guy blew up the house they'd been called to, but…

As if Cole had read her thoughts, he said, "I suspect the house explosion was as much a surprise to our man as it was to us. If he wanted you dead, he would've ordered the dog to go for your throat."

She flinched, and Cole winced. "Sorry. You didn't need to hear that, but if my theory's right, he's trying to terrorize you. Except the escalation in attacks has me worried, he's growing impatient with the game."

Game? Cole honestly thought some psycho was toying with her like a cat with a mouse? Could Luke's father be that sick? Could her colleagues?

Cole could've died in that house explosion. That dog could've torn Dan and the guy with the stick to pieces. How could she go back to work and put others in danger?

Except…

The image of Luke filled her vision, his last breath seeping from his lungs with his plea— *Don't forget your promise.*

She couldn't *not* go back.

Cole parked in front of Sherri's parents' house early the next morning. Masses of purple, pink and white overflowed the front flowerbeds, a colorful welcome banner against the backdrop of the yellow bungalow. The scent of fresh-cut grass and children's laughter drifted through the truck windows. Across the street a husband kissed his wife goodbye, next to a car packed with kids, triggering a twinge of longing that tightened Cole's chest.

Comforting Sherri yesterday morning, holding her close to his heart as if he had the right, as if she belonged in his arms, had turned his world upside down. For the past seven years he'd tried to convince himself that their youthful embrace hadn't been a world-tilting experience.

He'd been deluded.

But he couldn't let it happen again. She was a victim in a case he was investigating. He needed to adhere to professional boundaries.

Never mind that everything in him wanted to soothe away her pain. Still wanted to. He had no business entertaining romantic thoughts about her. She was still grieving for Luke. She'd clearly cared deeply for him. No doubt he'd been worthy of her affection. Cole glanced at his father's barren yard next door. Far more worthy than he could ever be.

The truck's passenger door suddenly burst open, and Sherri climbed in. "Have you been waiting long? I didn't hear you drive up."

"No, just got here. I'd intended to come in."

She reached for the folder in his hand. "It's probably better if we work somewhere else today. Are these the pictures of the frontline workers we narrowed in on?"

At the graze of her fingers, his insides jumped. He jerked back his hand and cleared his throat. "Yeah, the six likeliest are on top." For the better part of yesterday, they'd pored over staffing schedules of firefighters, paramedics and sheriff's deputies. They were the people most likely to know when Sherri would be in the next ambulance to be called to a scene and would know how best to manipulate paramedic protocol to their advantage.

After going back two months to try to find a pattern that fit with the timing of the attacks, they'd only found one definitive common factor—a woman, Bev Lucey, who'd been on dispatch at the time of every incident.

Sherri picked up the picture on the top of the stack. "This is Bev?"

"Yeah, you recognize her face?" Sherri hadn't recognized the name last night and they hadn't been able to find a picture of her online or find out much else about her even from her social media accounts, except that she'd moved to Stalwart and had started the job only a few months ago.

Sherri stared at the picture, cocking her head

one way, then the other. "No, I don't recognize her at all."

"Maybe we'll find a connection between her and one of the patients you've tended." Reviewing patients' names was on the top of today's to-do list after they finished with the pictures of the frontline workers. "Take a look at the rest of the photos. The next two are guys who were on duty at the same time as eighty percent of the incidents." Cole figured that one or two of the incidents could have been coincidences, accounting for the less than 100 percent.

Sherri leafed through the next three photos, shaking her head. "These are the three who were off duty when most of the incidents happened?"

"Yeah." He was leaning toward them since they would've been freer to make the bogus 9-1-1 calls. Cole glanced up at her parents' house. Her father stood at the window looking out at them. Then the curtain dropped back, shielding him from Cole's view. Yeah, Cole couldn't blame him for being watchful. If he had a daughter like Sherri, he wouldn't have even let her climb in his truck. Maybe she hadn't told them about his brother holding a knife to her throat.

He admired how she didn't seem to hold a grudge against Eddie, only wanted him to get well. Without thinking, he swept back the silky hair that cascaded off her shoulder as she bent over a photo. Snatching back his hand, he glanced back at the house and reminded himself not to admire anything else about her, because clearly her father wouldn't approve.

"Did Eddie recognize any of these guys?"

"No. I showed him the stack last night, but he said none of them looked like the guy who told him to raid your ambulance." Although, he wasn't 100 percent confident his brother had been telling the truth. When he'd first arrived at the house last night, Eddie wouldn't let him in because he'd still been steamed that Cole had turned in his phone. Dad had shown up as he'd searched under rocks for the spare key they used to keep in the flowerbed—when there'd actually been flowers in it.

Cole cringed at the memory of the "yeah" he'd choked out in response to Dad's "good to see you." He'd managed to avoid getting into anything deeper by saying, "I have photos Eddie needs to look at, and he's refusing to open the door."

To Cole's surprise, Dad had unlocked the door, snapped off the TV and ordered Eddie to look at the photos. Even more surprising had been his "Your brother was doing his job turning in your phone, and you should be helping him find this jerk any way you can."

With that Dad had left. But five minutes later,

he'd come back and handed Cole a mug of coffee and asked if Eddie had recognized anyone.

Cole had accepted the coffee, feeling like a traitor to Mom. But at least he'd stopped short of engaging in small talk by rushing out the second Eddie had exhausted the stack of photos.

Sherri continued flipping through photos, pausing only momentarily on each until she reached the middle of the stack. "I ticked off this guy one time a couple of months back." She turned the picture of a lanky firefighter Cole's way. "He was first on the scene, and I criticized him in front of his captain for unnecessarily moving a patient with possible spine injuries."

Cole took the picture and looked at the name on the back. *Ned Blum.* "Okay, we'll check on his connection with Bev and see what we can dig up on him."

"Shouldn't we show the picture to your brother again?"

"He's at school by now. Besides, he said the drug guy had a goatee and beer belly."

"It could've been a disguise."

"Yeah, but unfortunately Eddie probably wasn't in great mental condition to recognize that. I'll try to get a voice recording for him to listen to."

Sherri let out a sigh. "That would be easy enough to disguise, too."

His heart pinched at the resignation in her

voice, the dark circles under her eyes. "I could be off base with my theory that the guy manipulating Eddie was behind the attacks on you. His raid on your ambulance might not be connected to the other incidents."

"Then his appearance at the drug house the next night seems like a pretty big coincidence, don't you think?"

Yeah, never mind finding Eddie's phone in the woods at the site of the dog attack. He'd hesitated to mention that, afraid it would be the tipping point between her trusting him and not. He rammed his truck into Reverse and backed out of her driveway. "Let's ask your cousin Jake what he can tell us about Ned. He should know if he's the kind of guy who'd carry a grudge."

When they reached the fire station, Jake was outside polishing the fire engine, and Sherri jumped out of the truck before Cole could stop her.

Hopefully anyone noticing her arrival would think she was just paying her cousin a visit, not asking about suspects. Thankfully the rest of the crew appeared to be working inside the bay. Cole reached Sherri's side as Jake said, "No, Ned's pretty laid-back." He glanced at Cole and nodded. "We ribbed him about it, but he seemed more interested in scoring a date than getting even."

The hair on the back of Cole's neck prickled

at that news. "Did he ask you out?" If Sherri had rebuffed him after dressing him down, that could've provoked him.

Sherri looked stunned. "No. He's never talked to me."

Jake chuckled. "I'm not surprised. You don't exactly put out welcoming vibes where guys are concerned, if you know what I mean."

Sherri rolled her eyes as if she'd heard it all before, but that only worried Cole more. She could've rejected some screw-loose guy without even realizing it, and unrequited love was high on the list of triggers for stalkers.

Jake flicked a spray of water in Cole's face, pulling his attention away from the guys he'd been eyeballing in the bay. "Ned isn't behind the attacks, at least not the recent ones."

Cole narrowed his eyes at Jake. "How do you know?"

"He flew to Virginia last week. His father died. He's not due back for three more days. Have you considered unsatisfied customers? Sherri's bed-side manner isn't the sweetest."

Sherri jabbed his arm.

Jake balked. "See what I mean!"

"Yeah." Cole laughed. "We're reviewing that *massive* list of names today."

Sherri planted her hands on her hips with an unamused huff. "While you two do the male bonding thing at my expense, I'm going next door to grab a coffee."

"Good idea. I'll grab the list and we can go over it there."

As Cole reached inside his truck and pulled out his laptop bag, Jake lowered his voice and leaned in close. "I asked my dad to keep an eye on Luke's father. Check out who might be doing him any favors. But from the intel he's been able to gather, he says it doesn't look like Atkins is behind the attacks."

Cole nodded his thanks. Jake's father was the retired sheriff, and what he'd been able to learn unofficially in twenty-four hours was probably more than Cole could've learned in a week, with nothing but a hunch and a grieving father's misplaced blame to justify a warrant for phone and banking records. And without any concept of Bev Lucey's motivation, Cole wasn't likely to convince a judge to sign a warrant for her phone records simply because she happened to be on dispatch at the time of every incident involving Sherri.

Cole hurried across the parking lot to the coffee shop and spotted Sherri through the front window sitting at a booth. A good-looking guy stood beside her table, smiling down at her and nodding in response to something she said. By the time Cole stepped inside, the guy had slipped into the seat across from her and had her laughing. The sweet sound made Cole smile, and he couldn't help wishing he'd been the one to draw it out.

Her gaze lifted and connected with his. "Here he is now."

The guy shifted in his seat. "Morning, deputy." He touched the brim of his baseball cap.

"Morning." Cole wasn't wearing his uniform, which meant Sherri must've filled this guy in on why Cole was meeting her here. That surprised him, considering she'd been reluctant to even accept that she'd been a target. Was it to avoid a misunderstanding that they might be a couple? Was she attracted to this guy?

He stood, scooping up a takeout tray of coffees, and touched Sherri's arm that rested on the table. "Good talking to you. You take care."

Oh, yeah. This guy was into her. Cole's stomach knotted. He nodded to him as he left and then commandeered the seat he'd vacated. "Who was that guy?"

"Joe Martello. He's stopping by the ambulance base to visit the guys."

"Why?"

"They're old friends." She pushed a second mug of coffee across the table toward him. "Why are you all worked up? Did Jake say something more about Ned after I left?"

"No, I'm worked up because—" Cole glanced

at the nearby patrons and lowered his voice "—you told me you didn't have any wannabe boyfriends. Care to change that status report?"

She laughed, but it didn't sound nearly as sweet as her one for Joe. "Trust me. He is not a wannabe boyfriend."

"He's never asked you out?"

She glanced out the window at his departing back—a jock's back in designer clothes—and a smile played on her lips. "I suppose he did, once."

The amusement in her voice riled him beyond reason. "And you're telling me that fact didn't cross your mind when we were tabulating potential suspects?"

She blinked. "No, it didn't."

He reined in his rising voice. "I'm sorry. It's just…" Cole clamped his mouth shut. Was it jealousy that made him cringe at the fleeting touch Joe had given her before leaving?

Sherri shook her head, amusement dancing in her eyes as if she knew it. "It was over two years ago and only weeks after he got out of rehab. I'm sure he never really expected me to say yes. I politely declined and that was the end of it."

Cole squinted at her. "What do you mean he never expected you to say yes? Guys don't ask women out if they know they're going to get shot down."

She bobbed her head as if not quite ready to

agree. "I hadn't exactly been his favorite person, but maybe rehab had made him see that I should've been."

"What's that supposed to mean?"

Sherri sipped her coffee, her gaze shuttered.

"Sherri?"

Blowing out a heavy sigh, she set down her coffee. "He was my first partner. His wife left him and he started drinking heavily, maybe even taking drugs. It started to affect his work. The day his wife remarried, he showed up drunk to work. I reported him to our boss. He was fired soon after."

Cole gaped at her. "And you didn't tell me this, why?" He couldn't keep the irritation out of his voice, but he managed to haul it down a dozen decibels before continuing. "I can't think of a better motive than that for wanting to terrorize you."

Sherri paled. "But…" She glanced out the window then at her trembling hands. She jerked them beneath the table. "But that was three years ago. He's better now. He's sober. Has a great job, if his new SUV and designer clothes are anything to go by. And he looks fitter than I've ever seen him. I don't run into him often, but when I have he's always been friendly. I doubt he'd ever say so, but my reporting him was probably the best thing that ever happened to him."

Cole downed a gulp of the black coffee to give

himself a chance to rein in the are-you-really-that-naive lecture burning his lips. "As true as that might be, no guy appreciates being fired, however good the end result. And absolutely no guy enjoys putting himself out there to be shot down. You burned him twice. He's worth looking into."

Sherri visibly squirmed. "If he was that mad don't you think he would've taken revenge years ago?"

Cole clenched his jaw, thinking about how many years he'd stewed over what Dad had done to Mom. It'd only made the anger intensify, not lessen, especially as each year passed by with scarcely an attempt on Dad's part to make amends. "Not necessarily. We'll go through the list of patients' names like we planned and see if any names pop, but then I'm going to dig into your former partner's activities. Find out if he's friendly with our dispatcher."

"Please don't confront him directly. If he thinks I've accused him, he'll go ballistic."

"Oh?" he said wryly. "I thought he was charmed by you?"

She snorted and resumed sipping her coffee.

"Sounds to me like you already know he's capable of pulling these stunts."

"No, he's changed. It's just he said all kinds of nasty things to me after I reported him and he lost his job. And it was hard on my colleagues, because they were old friends and I'd broken some brotherhood code by snitching on him, even though deep down I'm sure they knew I'd done the right thing."

Yet another reason why she'd been so quick to suspect her colleagues. So why not her former partner? "In all our brainstorming of people with motivation to torment you, Joe honestly never occurred to you?"

"No. This stuff only started happening in the last couple of months. We weren't looking much further back than that. And I can't remember the last time I've seen Joe."

"But now…? You've got to agree he's our prime suspect. He knows the protocol, would know better than anyone ways to make you look bad or to frighten you while still making it look like it's all a coincidence."

"Sure, I guess. But if it's not him, I don't want him hearing that he was under suspicion, or he'll hate me all over again."

Cole bristled at the admission that the man had hated her. Certain he was their man, Cole sped through the review of her ambulance logs in the couple of months prior to the start of the incidents. Beside Reinhart, who he'd already eliminated, along with his son, since the latter hadn't been in the area in the past two months, Sherri put forward only three other possibilities. "Okay,

I'll run background checks on these and check on connections to our dispatcher and then get back to you."

"Can't I help?"

"At this point I need to do face-to-face interviews. It's probably better if you're not seen."

She looked almost relieved. She had another week of medical leave before her stitches would be healed enough for her to return to work. And hopefully he'd have enough to make an arrest before then. "C'mon, I'll drive you back to your parents'."

"Just so you know, I told my mom and dad that I was moving back to my apartment tonight."

"Why?" Cole wrestled down his uneasiness with the idea, knowing she wouldn't want to hear it, and worse than that, pretty sure hearing it would only make her more determined.

"I need to." Her tone confirmed it wasn't open for discussion.

"Let me know if you go out." It was an order, not a question. "I can arrange extra patrols. And it'd be a good idea not to go out alone if it can be helped."

"I run every morning on the river trail. Well, it'll be a walk until the stitches heal a little more."

"Call me and I'll accompany you."

"But all the incidents happened when I was on the job."

"And maybe the guy will stick to that pattern. Maybe he won't," Cole said sternly. "It's not a chance I'm willing to take. Are you?"

She looked up, a stubborn glint in her eyes. She was too headstrong for her own good.

"If you don't promise to call me—" he sipped his coffee, then slowly set the cup down "—I'll camp outside your apartment, if that's what it takes to keep you safe."

Her jaw dropped open, bobbed shut. Then she emitted a nervous-sounding laugh, clearly not sure what to read into the ultimatum.

Not wanting to examine his motives too closely himself, he raised his eyebrow to let her know he was waiting for her promise.

"Okay, yes, I promise to call you before I go out anywhere." She let out a little huff. "Happy?"

Ridiculously.

EIGHT

Stepping out of her favorite boutique, Sherri slung her shopping bag over her good shoulder and gave her new cousin-in-law a sideways hug. "I needed this. Thanks for dragging me out." Being cooped up in her apartment for the past week had been pure torture.

Well, except for the morning jogs with Cole.

Kara returned her hug. "Anytime. Besides—" Kara's voice dropped conspiratorially "—you weren't the only one who needed new clothes."

Sherri laughed. "But your reason is so much better!" Kara had confided that she and Jake were expecting. Buying new clothes to accommodate an expanding waistline beat opting for loose-fitting blouses over tank tops to hide an ugly dog bite any day.

Kara frowned. "Does the wound still hurt?"

"No." She quickly dropped her hand, realizing she'd self-consciously palmed her shoulder. "I'm back to work tomorrow." Thank goodness. She missed the distraction of work. Her nightmares had taken on a whole new level of horror, with savage dogs and drug-house booby traps added to her desperate efforts to save Luke.

Her heart stuttered. Yes, she wanted to be working, but what if the attacks started again?

Cole hadn't found anything that linked their suspect dispatcher to any of her disgruntled patients or to Joe. And Joe's employer wouldn't share Joe's schedule, so Cole hadn't been able to compare it to the times of the various incidents. She hoped Joe's boss could be trusted to keep the request confidential.

Gulping, she glanced over her shoulder and then scanned the cars parked along the curb and the shoppers strolling the street.

"Don't push yourself too hard, Sherri. You don't have to prove yourself to anyone."

Maybe not. But none of the guys wanted her back at work. And what little satisfaction she'd gotten from refusing to bend to their pressure tactics had withered with Cole's doubts that they were behind the incidents.

Kara stopped in front of the bakery window and inhaled. "The baby thinks it's time to eat."

Sherri burst into a much-needed giggle. "Oh, you're going to love using that excuse on Jake, aren't you?" She peered in at the tempting treats and noticed a reflection of someone watching her. She whirled around.

The man slipped into the hardware store across the street.

"What's wrong?" Kara tracked the direction of her gaze and Sherri suddenly felt foolish.

"Uh, nothing. I just thought I saw someone I knew." Except it wasn't Cole. The build had been too slight. "Let's go in and treat ourselves to a doughnut."

"Yes, my treat."

As Kara labored over her choice of flavors, Sherri edged to the front window and scanned the other side of the street again. When she'd told Cole about her Main Street shopping trip with Kara, he'd said he'd make extra patrols in the area. He'd sounded so concerned. Maybe he'd sent out an undercover guy. After all, any guy who'd change his morning routine and meet her at the river trailhead at seven sharp every morning to ensure she didn't jog alone wasn't likely to rest easy over her going shopping. Only, no one seemed to be paying particular attention to the bakery shop. She peered up and down the street. Maybe all this talk about the attacks just had her spooked.

"What kind do you want?" Kara called over to her.

"Apple fritter."

"You always get that. You should try something new."

Sherri shook her head and accepted the fritter from the clerk. "I like to stick to what I know." An image of Cole inexplicably flashed through her mind. Hiding a secret smile, she sank her teeth into the confectionery. Yeah, she knew Cole. It may have taken him seven years to get his feet squarely underneath him, but he'd grown into a caring, protective man. The kind of man who could sweep her off her feet if she wasn't careful.

Except when she saw how deliriously happy Kara looked with her hand straying to her scarcely bulging tummy every few minutes, Sherri didn't want to be careful. She wanted to let herself fall in love. Get married. Have a family.

Kara nudged her arm. "You know, with all this time you've had off, we should have gone on a double date. Maybe with that deputy whose been joining you on your morning jogs?" Her voice rose suggestively.

Sherri rolled her eyes. "He's investigating my case, not dating me." Cole had kept his professional distance since comforting her in the cemetery, but from the softness in his gaze when he looked at her, she liked to think his caution had more to do with not wanting to get kicked off the case. And that she hadn't exactly invited any more hugs.

Kara laughed. "But you wish he would." She drew out the last word in a lyrical tease.

Sherri's face heated. Was she that easy to read? She'd had a crush on Cole forever and the man version was a hundred times more attractive, from his chiseled good looks to his strong arms to his fierce protectiveness.

She turned to the door. She'd been operating on the premise that if she hid her emotions, no one could use them against her. Except Cole hadn't used her breakdown at the cemetery against her. Maybe she could open up a little more. What was the worst that could happen?

The fritter turned to dust in her mouth. He'd find out she was an emotional wreck. And get her kicked out of her job and then leave her again.

Sherri yanked open the bakery door, feeling suddenly claustrophobic. Except would he leave again?

The man who had held her in the cemetery and asked about Luke, hadn't seemed like the kind of man who'd walk away. A chill shivered down her spine and she instinctively backed up, bumping Kara's arm.

Kara fumbled her doughnut, nearly losing it. "What's wrong?"

"Uh—" Sherri scanned the street and shop

windows she couldn't see through. "Nothing. It was nothing."

Cole cruised slowly past in his patrol car and waved.

Smiling giddily, she waved back, taking more pleasure than she should in her apparent sixth sense of his nearness.

"Hey!" A man called from across the street. It was the guy who'd tried to save her from the dog. He dodged traffic to get to her. "How's the shoulder?"

"Better. Thanks to you." She turned to Kara. "This is the guy I was telling you about, who pulled the rodeo-clown routine on that dog."

He extended his hand to Kara. "Hi, the name's Ted." His warm gaze returned to Sherri as he released Kara's hand and touched Sherri's arm. "I'm just glad I was there. When are you back to work?"

"Tomorrow."

"Well, you take care." He dipped his chin to Kara. "Nice meeting you."

"Wow, he seems nice." Kara waggled her eyebrows. "If I wasn't already married to the best guy in town, I wouldn't mind being rescued by a guy like him."

Sherri scratched at her scar. "Trust me. It's not worth it."

Kara shrugged, a twinkle in her eye. "You're

forgetting that I married the man who rescued me." She led the way down the street and motioned to the fire station. "Mind if we stop in and say hi to Jake?"

"No problem. You go ahead. I wouldn't mind dropping by the ambulance base." Sherri skirted the fire station and headed for the ambulance bays in the lot behind.

"Hey," Dan said as she stuck her head into the lounge. He slanted a guilty glance at Joe, and then headed her off, steering her back into the hall. "I thought you weren't due back until tomorrow."

"I'm not." She held up her bag, wondering if Cole knew Joe was here again. "I was out shopping and thought I'd say hi."

"I guess you heard that they confirmed the bogus 9-1-1 call came from that cell phone Cole found?"

"No, I didn't hear anything about a phone." Her hopes rose. "Do they know who it belongs to?"

Dan snickered. "Yeah, I should've figured he wouldn't tell you. The guy shouldn't be on the case. He's been grilling the rest of us as if *we'd* pull these stunts. Or Luke's father. Can you believe the nerve?"

Her pulse quickened. If not for Cole's tenacity, there wouldn't be a case. "Who made the call?"

Compassion filled Dan's eyes, quickly replaced by irritation as he raked his hand over his whiskers, looking like he didn't want to be the one to tell her. "That punk brother of his."

"What?" The image flashed through her mind of Eddie hunched outside the ambulance after he caught sight of her wound. *Looking guilty?*

Dan squeezed her arm. "I'm sorry. I know you didn't want it to be him."

She sloughed off his touch. "Excuse me. I have to go." She stormed out the door and veered across the parking lot toward the sheriff's office. No wonder their leads had dried up. Even Cole's supposed suspicions of Joe. He'd just been pretending to investigate. Probably just pretending to care about her, too, to dupe her into trusting him.

"Hey, wait up." Kara hurried out the side door of the fire station.

Sherri pressed her shopping bag into Kara's hand. "Take this and go visit longer with Jake. I need to talk to Cole. Alone."

Kara took the bag, looking worried. "Want to talk about it first?"

"No. This is between me and Cole."

He was stepping out of a cruiser when she stalked up to the station. He took one glance at her and said to his partner, "Go on in. I'll catch up with you in a minute."

She closed the distance between them in three long strides and didn't bother waiting until Zeke was out of earshot before she drilled a finger into

Cole's chest. "What are you playing at, Cole Andrew Donovan?" Thinking, for the first time in her life, that his initials suited him all too well. He was a cad, with a capital *C*.

The light blinked out of his eyes. "You heard about the cell phone." He sounded disappointed or maybe resigned.

"Yes, and I'm wondering why I didn't hear about it from you." She poked his chest. "Did you think I wouldn't find out?" Thank goodness she hadn't actually started opening up to him. Clearly she couldn't be open and honest with a man hiding facts from her.

He enclosed her hand in his and drew closer. "I was going to tell you."

She wavered, foolishly wanting to believe him. No, she'd already made that mistake. She snapped her hand from his grasp. "Sure you were. Right after you helped your brother skip town. Or clouded the case with so many suspects he'd never be convicted." And to think she'd helped by dreaming up other potential suspects for him to harass.

And that he'd blatantly carried on the ruse by insisting on joining her on her jogs every morning. Keeping her running scared when all he had to do was watch his brother.

"My brother didn't make the call. Yes, it was his phone. But he had lost it over a week before. I swear to you he was with me when that call came through. He didn't make it."

She shook her head, her gaze fixed on his moving lips, but scarcely registering his words. Not that it mattered. She couldn't trust what came out of his mouth. "Why did you take this case?" She hated how her voice cracked.

"Because it kills me to see someone trying to hurt you. Sherri, I promise you, I—"

She sliced her hand through the air. "Stop! I don't want to hear your promises." She yanked her shirt collar sideways to expose her shoulder. "Did you get a good look at what that dog did to me? What kind of sick loyalty lets—?"

She stopped as his face turned pasty, his gaze fixed on the jagged scar, his throat convulsing as if he might throw up. Yeah, nice to know that was the kind of reaction she could look forward to from here on out if she ever decided to flash her shoulder at a guy.

"I'd never hurt you," he whispered, his gaze lifting to meet hers. "You've got to know that."

"Right, because your leaving seven years ago never hurt. Never mind that you never called. Never wrote." She clamped her mouth shut. He'd never given her any reason to think he would, not really, unless you counted his innocent kiss or the way he'd hugged her afterward or the gift he'd given her when he left.

Pain shadowed his eyes. Eyes she'd once believed she'd never tire of gazing into, of tracing the dark blue and white rays that burst from his huge pupils like rays of sunshine. "Please, you've got to trust me."

She broke the hypnotic grip of his gaze and turned on her heel. "No, I don't."

Cole braced for round two as Sherri whirled straight into her firefighter cousin's chest.

"Whoa, you okay?" Jake caught her by the elbows and searched her face.

She blinked rapidly and let out a lousy impersonation of a laugh. "Of course, why wouldn't I be? Excuse me." She strode across the street toward the woman Cole had seen her shopping with earlier, who'd apparently also been watching the spectacle.

Cole cringed to see that the woman hadn't been the only one. A couple of paramedics outside the ambulance bay were gawking, and Zeke had parked himself on a bench outside the sheriff's office.

Cole returned his attention to Jake, who'd leaned back against Cole's truck and perched his elbows on the hood, stretching his long legs in front of him as if he were there to shoot the breeze, not read him the riot act.

Yeah, fat chance. Cole remembered Sherri telling him once that she'd never been lonely having no brothers and sisters, because she had so many cousins. And Jake was clearly playing the big-brother role today.

"What did you say to her?"

"Not enough." Not that pointing out he'd thrown his brother under the bus by turning in that phone would've made any difference.

Jake chuckled. "Oh, I don't know."

"Pardon me?" Cole squinted at him. What kind of big-brother cousin was he?

"I saw the blowup from across the street."

Him and everyone else. "Don't worry, I have no intention of—"

"Whoa, stop right there. I didn't come over here to tell you to stay away from her." He slanted a glance her way. "Just the opposite." His palm circled over his clenched fist. "She'd pummel me if she knew I was asking. But I was hoping you could help her."

Still a little stunned that Jake *wasn't* there to pummel him, Cole plunged his hands into his pockets. "Trust me. I've been following every lead I can muster. That's why I turned in Eddie's phone. And now neither of them trusts me. The only reason the sheriff hasn't kicked me off the case is because he's short-handed with guys on vacation and he probably knows Zeke'll nail me to the wall if I show any favoritism to my brother."

"I meant help her personally."

Cole's heart hammered. *Personally?*

"I don't have to be a rocket scientist to see you care about her." Jake went on as if his request hadn't dropped a twenty-story elevator out from under Cole.

Sherri deserved a lot better than him. Frankly, he was surprised Jake hadn't already figured that out. As attracted as Cole was to Sherri, in addition to his inexplicable, soul-deep need to comfort and protect her, he couldn't mislead her. He'd seen firsthand how his dad had crushed Mom. And he never wanted to be responsible for inflicting that kind of pain. He'd clearly already given her false hope seven years ago without even realizing it.

"You know Sherri," Jake went on. "She's never been the emotional type. On the job, she's been an Ice Queen since day one. You know how it goes. We have to compartmentalize our emotions to survive the work."

Cole's thoughts flashed to the night at the drug house. Fire—not ice—had flared in Sherri's eyes when she'd treated him.

"Whenever anyone in the family tries to talk to her about what's going on, she sloughs off our concerns. She doesn't have a healthy enough fear of this crackpot making the crank 9-1-1 calls on her watch. And if she's convinced herself it was your brother, she'll have even less."

"But how am I supposed to talk any sense into her? She doesn't believe I'm telling the truth about my brother."

"If anyone can, you can. You're the first person I've seen get a rise out of her in months."

Cole's heart pitch-poled over a full three beats. "In months?" His mind flashed to the nightmare he'd witnessed her having at the hospital—the one he'd assumed was a reaction to the dog attack, until she'd cried Luke's name. The same as his mom used to do. His mother had shut down emotionally after Dad had cheated on her. She'd boxed up her feelings so tightly that Cole hadn't had a clue to how traumatized she'd been until the nightmares had started. "You mean *months*, as in since her partner *died*?" he asked pointedly.

Jake gaped at him for an unbearably long second, then groaned, a look of total self-recrimination sweeping over his face. "How did I miss that? Of all people? With what I went through after losing my first wife the way I did, I should've…" He shook his head. "Yeah, it has been since she lost Luke."

Cole winced at how intimate that sounded. Not "since she lost her partner" or "after Luke died," but "since she lost Luke," as if Luke definitely had been more than a partner.

* * *

Lost Luke. Cole jammed his time card into the slot, annoyed that three hours later Jake's words still grated against his emotions. What difference was it to him if she'd been in love with her partner? He'd already thought as much when she'd cried in his arms at the cemetery.

Cole grabbed his jacket and plodded to his truck. It wasn't as if he had any hope of winning Sherri's heart. Or should have.

She didn't even trust him. Not anymore. He rammed the stick shift into Reverse and squealed out of the parking lot. Okay, considering his brother had held a knife to her throat, who could blame her?

But her cousin had been right about one thing. If she convinced herself that he and Eddie were the bad guys, she might stop taking extra precautions, and the real stalker could blindside her in a heartbeat.

And he couldn't let that happen.

He turned toward her apartment. Zeke's jeep slithered around the corner behind him. Cole wasn't sure where his partner lived, but somehow he doubted this was his usual route home. As Cole parked in front of Sherri's redbrick building, the man drove by with a wave.

What were the chances he didn't know this was Sherri's place? If he'd heard half of what Jake had said, then chances were next to none. Zeke was bound to manufacture implications of Cole's after-hours visit to suit his own agenda.

Yanking the keys from his ignition, Cole jumped from the truck. Let Zeke say what he liked. Sherri's safety was all that mattered.

Movement snapped his attention to the far front corner of the four-unit building. A medium-build male skirted through the flowerbeds and disappeared behind the building.

Cole darted after him and at the corner, plunged through the flowers himself to peer down the adjoining wall undetected.

The guy had his face pressed to a window. One of Sherri's windows.

Cole stormed around the corner and caught the Peeping Tom by the shoulder. "What do you think you're doing?" Cole hauled him back and spun him around. "Ted? What are you doing here?"

The man whipped his arms in a circle, breaking Cole's hold and lunged for the next window. This one with only a screen between him and the inside. "I've got to get in there. She needs help."

A shriek came from inside her apartment. "No, stop!"

NINE

That was Sherri! Cole flung Ted aside and quickly scanned the empty bedroom. Seeing no one, he tore off the screen and vaulted inside.

The bedroom door opened to a short hall with two doors off it—a bathroom and another bedroom. The end of the hall opened to an entranceway to the right and a living room to the left. He strained to hear a telltale sound of which room she was in.

"You can't die, Cole," she shrieked from the direction of the living room.

He bolted down the hall, only registering the oddity of what she'd said as he rounded the corner and skidded to a stop at the foot of her sofa where she was wrestling with a blanket, her eyes scrunched tightly closed. Kneeling beside her, he gently brushed back strands of hair whipped across her face by her thrashing.

"Sherri, it's okay. It's just a dream."

Her limbs stilled, but the jerky movements

beneath her eyelids said she was still in the throes of the dream.

She had to be reliving the night outside the drug house. Her "you can't die" plea echoed in his mind as the tension began to leach from her face. He stroked the creases carved in her cheeks from the blanket, his heart turning soft and gooey. He'd come here to scare some sense into her, but seeing her look so vulnerable, he knew he couldn't do it. He wanted to take her nightmares away, not add to them.

Ted burst around the corner. "Is she okay?"

Cole whirled toward him. "What are you doing in here?"

Sherri awoke with a startled cry and levered to a sitting position. The instant her gaze collided with theirs, she shrank into the corner of the sofa, her eyes glassy. "How'd you get in here?"

"I heard you scream," he and Ted responded as one. Only Ted wasn't looking at her. His gaze slid intently about the room from the Bible and mystery novel on the end table to the framed jigsaw puzzles decorating the walls to the half-finished puzzle on the table at the far end of the L-shaped area, the changing nuances in his expression sending an uneasy feeling crawling over Cole's flesh.

He grabbed Ted by the collar and pinned him to the wall. "How'd you know it was Sherri screaming? How did you know she lived here? What are you doing hanging around her place?"

His hands shot into the air. "Protecting her." His voice pitched higher—the freaked-out pitch of a delusional mental patient. "I'm protecting her."

Sherri sprang to her feet. "Cole, let him go. You're hurting him."

Cole shot a searing glance over his shoulder, but she stood her ground.

"If he wanted to hurt me, he wouldn't have saved my life from that dog."

Pursing his lips to stop himself from saying something he'd regret, Cole refocused on the man's reddening face and eased his grip. "He was breaking into your house. We don't know what he might've done if I hadn't shown up."

"I wasn't breaking in," Ted argued, straightening his glasses. "I followed *you* in."

"You were peeping in her window," Cole growled, half-inclined to charge him for it.

Sherri's face blanched. "You were at my window?"

Cole gritted his teeth. This was not how he wanted to scare Sherri into being on her guard.

"I heard you cry out," Ted said, sounding sincere. "I thought you were in trouble."

From the tension radiating off Sherri, she didn't look convinced.

Cole gave him a hard shake. "You never answered my question. How did you know where she lived?"

His gaze darted about the room. "I didn't know. I live around the corner and was out walking. Heard her scream."

Cole's grip loosened, his mind harking back to what Ted had said when Cole had found him outside her apartment window. *I've got to get in there. She needs help.* He'd never said her name. Was it a coincidence? Was he just the kind of guy who rushed to help a damsel in distress?

"All right, you've seen she's safe. Now you need to go." Cole pushed him toward the door, intending to run a background check and surveillance as soon as he was through here. After the shock of Ted's appearance in her living room, he should at least have an easier time ensuring Sherri continued to take precautions. But first, he needed to get her to talk about the nightmare. Because between the nightmares and the general emotional shutdown her cousin had observed, Cole had a bad feeling she was in worse shape than either of them had thought.

Sherri held the door, waiting for Cole to leave with Ted.

Cole braced his palm against the wall, making no move to do so. "We need to talk before I go."

"Don't you think you should follow him?" She recalled the creepy-crawly-being-watched twinge she'd felt while out with Kara, minutes before Ted had crossed the street to greet her. Had he been watching her? "I think he lied about not following me home. He spotted me on the street today. Came up and asked how I was doing."

Cole reached for the door, but before she could exhale a relieved sigh, he closed it without leaving. "You don't have to worry about him. I'll make sure he doesn't bother you again." Cole's voice softened. "He's not what we need to talk about."

Remembering the nightmare Cole had walked in on, she scrambled for a way to avoid going there and blurted, "I was wrong earlier. I overreacted." That had to be why he'd come here in the first place—her reaction over Eddie's phone. "After I confronted you Kara pointed out that the fact you'd turned in Eddie's phone instead of hiding it proved you weren't trying to get him off the hook."

Cole's gaze looked pained. "That's not what we need to talk about."

"But…" She turned away, afraid of what he'd see if he looked too closely into her eyes. In her dreams, sometimes it was Cole, not Luke, who would be lying on the porch, bleeding out. She'd resist waking and drop back into the middle of the dream again and again, desperate to do things differently so he wouldn't die, until she'd finally come to her senses and fling herself out of bed to make the dream stop. "My blowup over Eddie is why you came, isn't it?"

"Actually, I came to ensure you don't let down your guard."

"Well, after this—" she strode to her bedroom, slammed shut the window and secured the lock "—I can assure you my guard is up." She shooed him back to the living room and double checked those windows.

"I'll cut you some two-by-fours to wedge between the sash and frame."

She wrapped her arms around her middle. "Thank you."

"You have a tape measure?"

"In the drawer of that end table there." With how much trouble she had getting to sleep at night, she couldn't believe she'd nodded off. Now, on top of not wanting to sleep for the nightmares, she'd never be able to close her eyes without worrying about someone breaking in.

Cole's muscles rippled beneath his shirt as he stretched the tape measure to the top of the window.

Waking up to him in her living room had been startling enough. Despite how, for the briefest moment, it had felt like the most natural thing in the world to see him the moment she opened her eyes.

Waking up to Ted would've been absolutely freaky.

She shuddered and had to admit she was glad Cole hadn't left right away. Except too big a part of her wanted to walk into his arms and feel them close protectively around her one more time.

He turned, caught her staring at him.

"Can I get you a lemonade?" she blurted.

"That'd be great, thanks."

She whirled toward the kitchen, banged her shin on a dining chair, knocked into the jigsaw puzzle she'd been working on and disappeared into the adjoining galley kitchen. How could she seesaw in mere hours from not trusting him to these...these feelings?

It had to be the adrenaline of the dream and waking up to find him hovering over her.

If he had an inkling of how messed up she really was he'd be leaving as fast as he could before she got the wrong idea about his concern for her welfare. Maybe if she let him have his say he wouldn't repeat what he'd witnessed to anyone else.

Dropping ice into glasses, she peeked around the wall separating the kitchen from the living room.

His gaze traveled over her mismatched secondhand furniture, the shabby table lamps, the framed puzzles depicting everything from air balloons to mountain scenes, and she wondered what he was thinking. She'd moved into the apartment only a week before Luke's death. Afterward, sprucing it up hadn't been high on her priority list.

His eyes brightened when they reached the stack of jigsaw puzzle boxes on the dining table. He walked over to them and studied the pictures one after the other. He paused on the box with the picture of a teddy bear in a nurse's cap bandaging another bear's paw.

Butterflies swooped through her tummy. He'd given her the puzzle the day before he'd left for college. Said he'd found it at a garage sale and that it had made him think of her. The fact that he'd bought a gift for her had been enough to make her silly teenage heart soar for months.

He set the box on top of the stack. "You kept it," he said, his voice husky.

Her heart did a ridiculous somersault. When months and then years had gone by without him coming home, she'd stuffed away her silly dreams along with the box. But she'd never quite been able to throw away the puzzle. "Mom brought those out when I was at the house. She thought they'd be a good distraction while I recuperate."

Of course, she'd avoided the teddy bear puzzle. Some wounds were better left scabbed over.

She splashed lemonade into the glasses. Okay, so maybe she'd never quite stopped hoping that one day he'd suddenly wake up and realize he was in love with her. But she wasn't the reason he'd come back to Stalwart. And really…she scarcely knew him. She shoved the lemonade pitcher back into the fridge. A childhood crush was no basis for a lasting relationship.

Neither was his protecting her from some psycho stalker.

If she even had a stalker.

"You know—" she handed him a glass "—maybe I am Princess Dark Cloud like the guys tease. And bad things just *happen* to happen on my shifts."

"Have you forgotten that someone else was in those woods? And whistled for the dog?"

She gulped. *Oh, yeah.*

"And it's far too coincidental that he happened to drop my brother's cell phone." Cole sifted through the puzzle pieces scattered about the table and fitted one into the lake scene she'd been working on. "It was clearly a calculated move."

The ice in her glass rattled, betraying her trembling as she strained to make sense of what he was saying. "You think this guy deliberately set up your brother?" She pressed her glass to her chest. "Why? He had to know you wouldn't fall for it."

"Because Eddie is an easy scapegoat. Your partner was already accusing him to anyone who'd listen. What better way to muddy the investigation than to throw more suspicion where it already lay? Not to mention pushing for other suspects would reek of a cover up with Eddie being my brother."

Just like she'd accused. "I'm sorry I thought that."

"It was a natural conclusion to jump to and my fault for not telling you about the phone in the first place." Cole splayed his palm across the small of her back and nudged her toward the sofa.

Warmth slid through her the same as she'd felt when his voice had reached into her dream earlier.

"If you think about it," Cole continued, "everything points to a setup. First the guy tells Eddie that stealing drugs from your ambulance will be easy. Next he calls to tell him about the drug house, claiming he wants to make up for getting him in trouble, which puts Eddie in the vicinity when you run into the booby trap. Then he drops Eddie's phone in the woods to implicate him in the dog attack."

"If it's the same guy."

"It seems likely, don't you think?"

Taking a seat on the couch, she replayed the scenarios in her mind and had to admit it did. "Except he hadn't counted on Eddie being with you at the time," she whispered.

"Exactly." Cole snatched up a couple of coasters from the far end table, then sat in the armchair kitty corner to her and set his glass on the table beside them. "That was his critical mistake."

He took her glass and set it on the table. "How are you really doing?"

At the compassion in his voice, her gaze snapped to the table he'd grabbed the coasters from. She'd printed out a couple of articles on PTSD. Her pulse raced. *Where did I leave them? Had he seen them? Was that why he looked so worried? Except they weren't on the table. Thank goodness.* "What…what do you mean?" Her mind scrambled to recall where she'd left the papers as her gaze skittered over the tape measure Cole had left on the table. *The catchall drawer?* She scooped up the tape measure and edged open the drawer. *No papers. Whew!*

She swallowed the lump in her throat and slipped back into her seat. "My shoulder has healed nicely. I'm fine to return to work tomorrow."

"Are you?" His thumb tenderly stroked her fingers.

When had he taken her hand? She snatched

it back. "Of course I am." Why did she have to offer him lemonade? She should've shooed him out after assuring him she'd be on guard.

He didn't attempt to reclaim her hand, but leaned closer, his eyes going irresistibly soft. "Sherri, having nightmares after a traumatic event is normal."

Great, he was pitying her.

"Talking through them can ease the need for your subconscious to work through your fears while you're sleeping."

She forced out a laugh. "You sound like a psychology professor."

"I took a few extra courses on the subject hoping to help my mom."

"What happened to your mom?" she asked, latching on to the chance to get the focus off her.

His cheek muscle ticked. "The divorce put her emotions through the wringer."

Sherri's heart yo-yoed. She'd always adored his mother. And his father. He hadn't seemed like the kind of guy who'd cheat on his wife. *But that just goes to show how easy it is to make people see what you want them to see*—she tucked her trembling hand under her thigh—*unless they happened to catch you in the throes of a nightmare.*

"I'm sorry about your mom and I appreciate your concern, but I'm fine. I've scarcely had any nightmares about the dog attack." They'd started long before that.

Cole lifted his lemonade glass and took an inordinate amount of interest in the condensation pebbling on the sides. "It's not just the nightmares. When's the last time you've hung out with friends?"

"I've been working a lot of shifts to get the hours I need to apply for the flight medic opening."

"You're distancing yourself from family, too."

How would he...? She folded her arms. "What did Jake tell you?"

"That you've been detached. Uncommunicative."

All symptoms of PTSD. She shook off the thought, rolled her eyes and sprawled back against the couch. "I've been busy."

The muscle twitches in Cole's cheek grew more pronounced. "Why are you getting defensive? I'm trying to help you."

"By cataloging my social faux pas?"

He set down his glass. "No, Sherri...I think you might be suffering from PTSD."

"That's ridiculous." She sprang to her feet and scanned the dining-room table, the countertops. "Do I look depressed to you? I don't drink. I don't do drugs." She didn't have PTSD. He had to have spotted the article and just assumed.

She stalked down the hall to her bedroom where Cole had come in and scanned the night table and dresser. The PTSD article wasn't anywhere to be seen. So where had he gotten the idea from?

She jolted at her reflection in the dresser mirror—the sunken eyes, the purple smudges beneath them. She smoothed her sleep-mussed hair. Oh, this was worse than she'd thought. If he suspected after only a couple of weeks in town, how long before her boss clued in and took her off duty?

Cole sprang up from the armchair to go after her. Except…darkness crept into the edges of his vision and he crumpled to the floor with a thud.

"Cole!" Sherri skidded to her knees at his side, sounding as frantic as the rain lashing the windows. *Rain? When did it start raining?*

He blinked open his eyes. The doctor had warned him that head injuries could trigger delayed symptoms. Had he actually passed out?

"Cole, what's wrong?" The concern in Sherri's eyes made his heart hammer. Her fingertips found the pulse point at his wrist, sending tingles charging up his arms as her gaze shifted to her watch. "Your heart is racing."

He chuckled. "Yeah, having a gorgeous woman

fuss over him will do that to a guy." He turned onto his side to push to his feet.

"Whoa." She pushed his shoulder back to the floor. "What do you think you're doing? You need to lie still."

"I'm fine."

"You're not fine. You just passed out."

He wedged his elbows behind him to raise his head closer to her eye level. "I'm fine." But...*her* breathing didn't sound too good, and the fear that he'd heard in her voice when he came to had crept into her eyes. In her nightmare, she'd begged him not to die. Had finding him on the floor triggered a flashback?

"We'll see," she said. "A few simple tests should tell me if you need to go straight to the ER. First, can you tell me the date?"

He twisted his arm to capture her hand still resting at his wrist. "I'm sorry I upset you. That wasn't my intention."

She squeezed his hand. "I'm more concerned about you at the moment. Do you know the date?"

He rolled his eyes. "Okay, I'll make you a deal. I'll let you give me your tests, but in return, I want some honest answers to a few questions."

She slipped her hand free of his grasp, sat back on her heels and pulled the cardigan she must've grabbed from her bedroom across her middle.

For a long moment, she just stared at him. "What kind of questions?"

"For starters, I'd hoped you'd tell me about your nightmares. Just before I nudged you awake you'd been begging me not to die." Not the way he wanted to fill her dreams. "I thought if we talked about them, they might ease."

She gulped, her gaze shifting to the rain-splattered window. "Did talking about her nightmares help your mother?"

"Yes." He eased into a sitting position, not wanting to trigger another blackout. His head was pounding, but Sherri didn't need to know that just yet. "At first I ignored her cries in the middle of the night, assuming she'd be embarrassed, but after I finally got up one night and made her a cup of cocoa and urged her to talk, the nightmares began to let up."

A hopeful light flickered in Sherri's eyes. "Really?"

"Yes." He leaned back against the front of the armchair. "So what do you say you sip your lemonade and tell me about your dreams?"

She arched one eyebrow in a perfect imitation of his first-grade teacher's reaction when he'd thought he'd talked his way out of something.

Not good.

"What's the date?"

He grinned. "June fourteenth. My birthday is

June twenty-eighth. And in case you're interested, I love caramel and pecan-filled chocolates. Your birthday is May twelfth."

Her eyes widened.

"You shouldn't be so surprised. We were neighbors for how many years? Do you know how many little girl birthday parties you had in your backyard in that time?"

Her melodic laugh warmed him. "As I recall, you and your brother would always *happen* to lose a baseball over the fence at about the time the cake and ice cream were served."

"Yup." He winked. "Good times."

"Okay, stand up. Hold out your arms. Close your eyes. Touch one index finger to your nose. Then the other."

He obediently did as she asked, although he was pretty sure the test was for sobriety, not a concussion "Okay, your turn."

She closed her eyes and touched her nose.

"Very funny. That's not what I meant."

Her mouth quirked sideways. "If I tell you about the dreams, will you promise not to say anything about them to anyone else?"

"Of course."

She opened her catch-all drawer and fished out a small penlight. "Not to my family? Or to Jake? Or...to my boss?"

Ah. He was beginning to see what she'd really

been worried about with his PTSD theory—that she'd be forced to stay on leave if it proved true. He sat on the couch. "It's between you and me."

She silently considered his offer. At least he hoped that was what she was doing as she flicked the light across one of his eyes and then the other. "Because, like you said, nightmares are natural after a traumatic event. They don't mean I have PTSD."

"You have beautiful eyes," he interjected before he could censor the thought. Maybe that bonk on the head *was* worse than he'd thought.

The corners of her mouth tipped up. So apparently she didn't mind. She pocketed the penlight, seemingly satisfied with his response. "If I did have PTSD, I'd be avoiding activities similar to those that triggered the nightmare. Right?"

"Typically, that's true, yes." He had a bad feeling that he'd been closer to the truth than he'd realized. Could she have countered the most common reaction—avoidance of similar situations—by sheer willpower?

She relaxed and joined him on the couch. "Okay, then as long as you promise, I'll tell you."

"I promise," he said, and prayed he wouldn't regret it. She'd seemed to be functioning fine on the job. None of the other paramedics had made any disparaging comments about her competency.

If she'd suffered flashbacks or anything else on the job, surely someone would have noticed.

"And promise me you'll go see your doctor first thing tomorrow. We'll skip our morning jog. You shouldn't be doing anything more strenuous than pencil pushing if you're still getting headaches. I can't believe you didn't tell me. I never would've let you come with me."

Yeah, that's why he hadn't told her. "I promise."

"Okay." She sucked in a big breath and stared at her hands folded in her lap.

His arms ached to hold her, to ease the anxiety that had to be writhing her insides worse than she was twisting her hands. He cupped his hand over hers.

"The nightmares started after Luke's shooting. He was shot in the chest and in my nightmare his blood seeps over my hand as I try to stop it." She pressed a palm to the left side of her chest.

Cole recalled her doing the same thing when he'd asked about Luke in the hospital. Had she been having a flashback then?

"In reality, I didn't apply pressure to his wound for very long, because Luke said he could do it and he begged me to save the patient and her unborn child. The woman's husband had pushed her down the stairs then kicked her in the stomach and she was hemorrhaging badly."

"Did you save them?"

Sherri's hand dropped back to her lap along with her gaze. "Yes."

The deep sadness in her voice didn't match her answer, and he knew she was thinking about who she'd lost—Luke.

With another deep inhalation, her expression blanked. This must've been what Jake had been talking about. She seemed to stuff away all her emotions. He wanted to ask if she blamed herself for Luke's death, but was afraid the question would open up wounds best left alone. The silence lengthened and he waited, remembering how it had taken awhile for his mom to work up the courage to share.

Sherri finally continued. "After you got blown off your feet in the house explosion, the nightmares morphed. Sometimes you, not Luke, would be bleeding out on the patient's porch."

Cole groaned. She'd relayed the experience without emotion, but the flatness in her eyes betrayed her torment.

"Then after the dog attack, sometimes a dog would show up in the dream, too."

An image of the dog ripping into her shoulder flashed through his mind, and he shuddered.

"Yeah, not pretty. So you can hardly blame me for not wanting to burden my family with it, let alone talk to anyone else."

He squeezed her hand. "It's not a burden to me. Your trust is a gift."

A gorgeous blush bloomed on her cheeks. "Well, my boss wouldn't think so. He'd stop me from working, from doing what I'm supposed to be doing. And…" She fluttered her other hand. "Guys wouldn't exactly clamor to marry a woman who might whack him in the throes of a nightmare every night." She laughed on a huff of air, clearly trying to make light of her revelation now. But his expression must've given away where his mind had veered at "marry a woman," because her blush deepened. "Not that I think we'd…" She waved her hand as if to wipe out what she'd said, looking more flustered by the second. "I meant—"

He pressed a finger to her lips. "It's okay. I understand." Oh, wow, her lips were soft. And despite his vow to stay unattached, he suddenly had the indefensible impulse to kiss her. To wrap her in his arms and feel the steady beat of her heart against his. To hear her whisper his name in a contented sigh, because she knew he'd keep her safe.

TEN

Just before three the next day, Ted's vintage orange Chevy Nova pulled out of an apartment complex around the corner from Sherri's.

"That's his car." Cole pointed.

Zeke tailed it. The sunny day had been a quiet one for the sheriff's office, so Zeke hadn't balked at Cole's suggestion that they concentrate their patrols around Ted's neighborhood. In fact, from the zeal of his cat-and-mouse maneuvers through traffic, he looked as if he was enjoying himself. "You do know that unless an ambulance call came in that we didn't hear about, Ted's not going after Sherri."

Cole strained to see around a truck that had pulled in front of them. "I still want to know where he's going." What he really wanted was a look in the man's medical records. The odds that he'd happened to be walking past Sherri's apartment when she screamed were slim enough, but his intense gawking once inside had sent all Cole's alarms bells clanging.

Eight minutes later, Ted parked in front of the mall and stepped out of his car dressed in a custodian's uniform.

Zeke cruised slowly down the next lane. "Well, he won't be bothering Sherri for the next eight hours if he's reporting to work."

Cole swept his gaze across the store signs—fourteen on this side alone. "I don't know. A mall this size must have a large cleaning staff. Would be easy enough to slip away for an hour with no one the wiser."

Zeke snorted. "I'm telling you, your brother's the one we should be keeping an eye on. This guy didn't strike me as a mental case. The department didn't have a shred of paperwork on him."

"Doesn't mean he's not." The guy was fixated on Sherri. Of that much Cole was certain.

"Look at that." Zeke stopped the cruiser at the end of the lane closest to the main entrance and jutted his chin toward Ted swallowing an elderly woman in an exuberant hug outside the door. "I bet she can tell us all you want to know about him."

Cole shifted in his seat for a better look. "Do you know who she is?"

"Sure. Mrs. Eden, my favorite high school English teacher."

The idea that Zeke had a favorite teacher, let alone one who taught English, left Cole a little stunned.

"Didn't you have her?"

"No, I've never heard of her. She must've retired before I got to high school." His partner had a good ten years on him at least, but Ted didn't, so how'd he know the teacher?

Zeke whipped into a parking spot. "No problem. I'll ask her." The instant Ted disappeared into the mall, Zeke shoved open his door and headed off the elderly woman.

By the time Cole stepped up beside him, the woman was twittering about how wonderful Ted looked now that he'd gotten off the drugs and had put on weight.

"He almost died, you know. Oh, my. It was horrible. I lived next door to the family then and I still remember how hysterical his mother was as the paramedics worked on him."

At the word *paramedic*, Cole jumped into the conversation. "How long ago was that?"

The woman slanted a stupefied glance his way. "Were you one of my students?"

"No, ma'am."

"I didn't think you looked familiar."

"Do you recall how long ago Ted almost died?"

Her gaze drifted to the sky. "Three years ago

now, I think. He got addicted to painkillers after he hurt his knee playing basketball."

"Do you happen to recall if a female paramedic responded to that call?"

Mrs. Eden's wrinkles realigned into a beaming smile. "Oh, yes. Hers was the first face he saw when he came back to us. Made quite an impression. He talked about her for months."

Cole exchanged a victorious look with Zeke. This explained the man's obsession.

"His heart had stopped, you see." Mrs. Eden went on, "And she jolted him back to life with one of those defibrillators."

A report of a car accident came over Cole's radio, injuries reported, which meant an ambulance would be dispatched. Cole called in an estimated time of arrival of three minutes.

They thanked Mrs. Eden and hurried back to the cruiser. Zeke flipped on the sirens and swerved onto the street. "Sounds to me like Ted's more interested in being Sherri's protector than hurting her."

Yeah, which meant their best hope of nabbing the real creep was to tail her runs. Oddly, Zeke seemed as eager as he was to do it.

Six minutes later, they pulled into the grocery store parking lot where two paramedics already were helping a young female victim. Sherri wasn't one of them. The accident amounted to the driver's bumper tapping the cement abutment and triggering the airbag, which in turn had gashed her arm. There was no exterior damage worth noting. Zeke thumbed a text message into his cell phone as Cole wrote up a report.

"Is the other team back at the station?" Cole asked the paramedics.

"They were when we left. Been a dead day."

Dead was good if it meant Sherri was keeping out of trouble. A call crackled over Cole's radio. "Attention all units, 10-79 at East End Mall. All available units report in."

Bomb threat.

Sherri and Dan parked outside the mall's south entrance, and a mall security officer held open the door.

"The kid's in the food court. Straight ahead."

"Thanks." They rushed the gurney inside as curious shoppers scrambled out of their way. The going got slow as they neared the food court and a thickening crowd. "Make way. Let us through," Dan yelled.

"The paramedics are here," someone shouted and the crowd that had been circled around the victim parted like the Red Sea.

A frantic-looking teenage girl was kneeling beside a male, about eighteen, triggering memories of Sherri's frenzy after Cole's collapse last night. Her heart thumped at the thought of how that had transpired, but she didn't regret confiding in Cole. And he'd been right. She'd slept through the night without a single nightmare for the first time in months.

"You have to help him. He can't breathe," the girl said. "He's allergic to peanuts."

The boy, dressed in black jeans and a black T-shirt, was clasping his throat and gasping for air, although his color didn't indicate a lack of oxygen. Reaching his side, Sherri fixed her stethoscope into her ears and exchanged a skeptical look with Dan, who'd already grabbed the vial of epinephrine and a needle from the trauma bag.

A fire alarm sounded.

Sherri could scarcely hear her patient's breathing over the surge of blood pulsing past her ears, but the boy was definitely pulling in air. She scanned the faces of the people around her who were now breaking away from the scene. What had happened to the security guard?

A loud voice came over the PA. "We need to evacuate the building. Please proceed to the nearest exit in an orderly fashion."

Great.

"This is not a drill," the voice over the PA went on. "I repeat. This is not a drill." The alarm resumed its blare, and Sherri pivoted on her knee to tell Dan they should load the teen on the gurney.

Another kid shoved a cloth over Dan's mouth and shouted, "It's a bomb!"

"What are you doing?" Sherri clawed at the kid's hand and screamed for help as Dan went limp, but no one paid any attention.

Everyone started screaming. And racing for the exits. Everyone except the teens circled around her and Dan and their questionable patient.

Her throat closed up. *Oh, God, help us, please.*

The patient smashed his head into Sherri's nose and sent her reeling backward. Pain exploded in her head. Blood spurted from her nose. As she struggled to her knees the girl pounced on their trauma bag. The kid holding the cloth to Dan's face snapped a handcuff on Dan's wrist then shoved him under a table and snapped the other cuff to the table's center pole.

Two guys grabbed her hands and pinned them to the floor as another pawed at her pockets.

She thrashed and kicked and screamed.

The girl, who moments ago had been pleading with Sherri to save her friend, stomped on Sherri's stomach. "The vials are in her belt, idiot."

Sherri roared in pain as a blur of blue sprang at the girl.

The punks let go of Sherri's hands and she curled onto her side, clutching her stomach.

* * *

Cole tried to reach Sherri on her cell phone as their cruiser chewed up the five blocks back to the mall. Sirens rose up from every direction of the city, and he prayed that Sherri's ambulance wasn't one of them. "She's not answering."

"You thinking what I'm thinking?" Zeke asked.

"That we need to locate Ted?"

"Yeah."

By the time they reached the mall, frenzied shoppers were pouring out the doors.

Cole scanned the sea of faces. "It'll be impossible to find him in this crowd."

"His car's still where he parked it."

"Good. Does the department have bomb-sniffing dogs?"

"One." Zeke snaked their cruiser around the frantic shoppers, blipping the siren to get people to move out of the way. "But from the look of the frantic evacuation, mall staff have already located it or something suspicious." Zeke rammed the brake, and Cole grabbed the dash, his gaze slamming into that of a pigtailed girl standing frozen in the center of the roadway.

The sheriff himself snatched her up and pressed her into the arms of a screaming mother. Then, slapping the hood of their cruiser, he said, "Take the east entrance. Help get people calmed down."

"Has the bomb been located?"

"No, but after the fire alarm was pulled, someone yelled *bomb* and everyone panicked."

"We need to see the surveillance feeds," Cole said. "We think we know who's behind this."

The sheriff shot them a skeptical look, but must've seen Cole's certainty, because a heartbeat later, he said, "Okay, I'll let mall security know you're on your way. It's that door there. One flight down. And stay off your radios."

Radio silence was standard protocol with a bomb threat. They didn't want a radio transmission inadvertently setting off the bomb. Cole's mind flashed to last week's blast, and his steps faltered as not-so-phantom pain knifed through his skull. Gritting his teeth, he shoved through the crowds battling to exit.

"This way." Zeke pointed to a flight of stairs, but two steps down, he grabbed a hoodie-clad teen by the arm and spun him toward Cole. "Look who we have here."

"Eddie? What are you doing here? You're supposed to be in school."

Eddie jerked his arm from Zeke's hold and stuffed his hands into the front pocket of his hoodie. "School ended half an hour ago."

Gripped by the fear that the bomb threat was meant to lure Sherri into a trap, Cole yanked Eddie out of the flow of people. "Were you meeting that *guy*? Is he here?"

Eddie didn't meet Cole's gaze.

Cole gave him a hard shake and raised his voice. "Is he here?"

Eddie shrank back, his hands fisting in the hoodie's front pocket.

Suddenly, a different picture materialized in Cole's mind. *A drug buy.* He yanked Eddie's hands from his pocket, but it was empty. "Answer me."

"I was just hanging."

Zeke clapped Cole on the shoulder. "Unless the kid knows where the bomb is, he needs to get out." Zeke pointed to the glass doors that the last of the customers were scurrying through.

Eddie's face blanched "I don't know nothing about a bomb."

Cole released his brother. "Get out of here. Go home."

"C'mon." Zeke tugged Cole down the stairwell. "The caller said the bomb was set to blow at four."

Cole glanced at his watch. Twenty-three minutes.

Cole trailed Zeke into a room full of monitors being scanned by a mall security guard and a lone deputy. "You see who pulled the alarm?"

"No." The deputy fiddled with dials on the control panel. "I've been rewinding surveillance footage to five to ten minutes before the call came in to see if I could spot anyone abandoning a suspicious package."

"Good. We're looking for a lanky male custodian. Have you seen him or anyone acting suspicious?"

"Nah." The guard's gaze bobbed from the monitors to Zeke and back again. "Everyone's scrambling to get out."

Cole rewound a feed from the mall's south end.

"What are paramedics doing in there?" Zeke pointed to the monitor and snatched up his phone.

At the sight of Sherri and Dan pushing a gurney through the south entrance, Cole's heart chilled. "When was that image shot?"

The deputy squinted at the screen. "A couple of minutes before we received the bomb threat."

"Yeah," the security guard said. "We had a guy choking or something in the food court. Had to call 9-1-1."

Cole grabbed the joystick that remotely controlled the camera near the south entrance and panned it to the limit of its range. He couldn't see them anywhere. "Have they already left? Where were they headed?" Cole demanded.

"I, uh…" the guard stammered, his gaze shooting to Zeke, who was talking on the phone.

The deputy fast-forwarded the feed Cole had been rewinding. "They didn't leave the way they came in."

"Dispatch says they haven't reported back in," Zeke relayed. "The call was for an anaphylactic reaction in the food court area. They'll have a deputy sweep the area."

Cole scanned the labels under the TV screens, found the one marked Food Court. "The screen's black. Why's the screen black?"

The security officer flipped a couple of switches. "I don't know. It should be on. Someone must have covered it."

Cole raced out of the room.

"Where are you going?" Zeke shouted after him.

"To find her!"

Sherri's heart shattered at the sound of fists connecting with Cole's flesh. He'd taken down the girl like a flash of lightning, but the punks had tackled him just as quickly. Squinting at them, Sherri strained to climb out of her pain and help him—she blinked—not Cole? Ted?

The girl rolled to her feet and thrust vicious kicks at his head.

"Help," Sherri cried, but couldn't croak out a sound louder than a squeak. She felt around her belt for her radio. Where was it?

Dan stirred, let out a low moan.

Spying his radio on his hip, she clenched her

teeth against the pain and struggled to her knees to crawl to him.

"Smash his phone," one of the punks yelled at the girl, who redirected her kicks from Ted's head to a cell phone on the floor.

"C'mon, we got to get out of here," a kid sporting a backpack yelled.

The guy who'd been pretending to be in anaphylactic shock rammed one last hard jab into Ted's kidneys. "Cuff the woman."

The greasy-haired teen who'd pawed her pockets earlier turned back to her with an ugly gleam in his icy-blue eyes. He twirled a pair of cuffs around his index finger and sneered.

"You want to die beside your partner? No problem." He snapped open a cuff and lunged.

She rolled out of his reach and swung her leg, taking his legs out from under him.

His chin clipped the edge of the table as he went down. "Oh, you're going to pay for that," he roared, calling her obscene names as he scrambled after her. Then all of a sudden he flipped onto his back.

"Run!" Dan yelled and hinged up his leg for another kick at the guy.

Sherri lurched to her feet.

But her fake patient snatched up the cuffs and grabbed her wrist before she could so much as turn on her heel. She memorized his face—pug nose, yellow-brown eyes, scraggly blond hair, the faint trace of a scar on his upper lip.

"Hurry," the girl shouted at him, then looking around, added a note of fake hysteria to her voice. "There's a bomb. A bomb! We have to get out."

He shoved Sherri down, kneed her head under the table and cuffed her to the same pole as Dan. "C'mon," he said, grabbing his friend, who'd pinned Dan's free hand under his foot and was glaring at her as though he wanted blood. He spit in her face and then took off.

Dan tugged his cuffed wrist, clanging the cuffs uselessly against the metal pole. He rammed his shoulder up into the table as if he might shove it off the pole. Then pulled out his multipurpose tool and started sawing at the links. Sherri grabbed the radio from his belt and depressed the call button. "This is M2. We have two paramedics and—" she glanced at Ted's prone body "—an unconscious male trapped in the mall's food court. I repeat—"

"No, don't use the radio," Dan shouted. "It could trigger a—"

Blast!

ELEVEN

Fifty yards from the chest-high wall circling the food court, Cole dove for cover behind the nearest pillar. Smoke spewed through the air. He squinted in the direction the blast had sounded, but couldn't see any flames or structural damage. "Can you see where it originated?" he called to Zeke, who'd ducked for cover behind a kiosk.

"That trash can to the right of the food court, I think."

Were they looking at a smoke bomb? Something to cause panic, but no real harm? Or a teaser to something bigger?

Heart pounding, Cole stuck his head out from behind the pillar and squinted through the smoke. "I don't see Sherri and Dan. Do you?"

"No." Zeke sprinted to a nearby pillar, but shook his head from the new vantage point.

Cole checked in with the sheriff on his cell phone. "Did the paramedics get out?"

"Negative. Did you see where the explosion hit?"

"Next to the food court. A smoke bomb by the looks of it and no sign of the paramedics."

"I want you out of there. The next one may not be just smoke."

Cole's stomach bottomed out. *Sixty thousand square feet to search and Sherri could be anywhere.*

"I see their gurney." Zeke pointed to the far end of the food court.

Another boom split the air.

Zeke dove for cover once more. And…was that Sherri's cry?

"Get out of there," the sheriff repeated more adamantly.

Spotting fresh plumes of smoke spewing from another trash can, Cole stuffed the phone in his pocket and sprinted for the chest-high block barrier between him and the dining area. "Sherri? Dan? Are you here?"

A third boom drowned out any answer, and the sprinklers kicked in.

"Sherri!" Cole shouted, squinting through the spray of water.

"Cole! Cole! Over here."

He heard her but couldn't see her. Ducking behind the cover of the barrier, Cole drew his gun and motioned to Zeke to skirt it in the other direction.

"Cole?"

The fear in her voice gnawed at his heart. "I'm here," he assured, staying low as he hurried toward a break in the wall. "Are you alone? Where's Dan?"

"He's here, too. They handcuffed us to a table before they ran off."

Cole edged around the corner of the wall, wanting to get a visual of the area before he made himself a target. At the sight of Ted sprawled on the floor between the tables, pushing to his knees, Cole stepped into view. "Get back on the ground. Hands where I can see them."

"I didn't do anything," the man blurted, dropping his face back to the tile. "I was trying to help her."

"It's true." Sherri crab walked from under a table as far as her cuffed wrist would let her.

At the sight of her blood-crusted face, Cole's stomach roiled. He never should've let her out of his sight.

"A bunch of drug-seeking teens staged a peanut allergy," she went on.

Zeke rushed in and cuffed Ted anyway. "For all we know he was in on it or on the bomb threat, along with who knows how many others." Zeke's pointed look left no doubt he was thinking of Eddie, who they'd caught rushing out of the mall within minutes of the bomb threat. Zeke hauled

Ted to his feet and updated the sheriff over the phone as Cole unlocked Dan and Sherri's cuffs.

Visibly shaking, she massaged her chafed wrist, and Cole had to summon every ounce of self-control not to drag her into his arms as firefighters descended on the area. He clasped Sherri's arm and steered her through the maze of tables.

"We've got to get them out of here," he said to Zeke, who was demanding answers from their sputtering suspect. Sherri's partner snatched up the ransacked trauma bag and hurried after them.

"There was a girl, about fifteen, and at least three teen boys," Sherri relayed breathlessly, one hand swiping at the sprinkler water dousing her face, the other clutching her side. "I can describe two of them. Identify them if the mall's security cameras picked them up."

"First let's worry about getting you safely outside." After the horrors she'd just escaped, he couldn't believe she was thinking straight, let alone capable of identifying their suspects.

"Those punks knew what they were doing," Dan groused, stalking alongside them toward the exit. "The one kid almost killed me with an ether-saturated cloth or something. I was out before I knew what hit me."

"Between the surveillance tapes and your testimony and any prints they left on that bag of yours, we'll nail these guys."

"You won't get any prints," Dan said. "They were wearing surgical gloves. That's what tipped me off. That and the fact the kid who'd supposedly had the allergic reaction was clearly getting enough air."

The sheriff met them at the exit. "Get them in the ambulance and pull it to the edge of the cordoned-off area."

Crowds lined the yellow tape, morbidly watching them make their way to the ambulance. Cole scanned the faces, wondering if Sherri's stalker was among them, or if Ted had been behind today's attack.

The sheriff's gaze skittered over Sherri's bloodied face. "The sooner you and your partner can ID your assailants on the security footage, the sooner we can lock them up. Do you think you can—" he motioned awkwardly at her nose "—treat that on site?"

"I can take care of her." Dan pressed a key ring into Cole's hand. "You drive us where you need us."

Cole helped Sherri into the back of their rig and reluctantly relinquished her to Dan's care.

Zeke secured Ted to the gurney of a second ambulance and flagged Cole. "We need to talk."

Cole yanked open the driver's door to move

the ambulance closer to the command station. "Can you get another deputy to accompany our suspect to the hospital? We need to stick around to review surveillance tapes."

"I think I'd better accompany him. Ted says he took pics of the suspects on his phone. I radioed the deputies inside to look for it."

"That's good."

"Maybe." Zeke's voice dropped. "He says he has other photos at home that we might want Sherri to look at."

A disturbing feeling slithered through Cole's chest at the memory of the guy's too intense interest in the inside of Sherri's apartment. "What kind of photos?"

"He says he's been 'watching out for her'—" Zeke air-quoted "—for a while and started taking photos after your kid brother assaulted her."

Cole gritted his teeth at how much pleasure Zeke clearly took in bringing up that connection. Cole jammed the keys into the ignition, ticked with himself for not pressing Ted harder about what he'd been doing outside Sherri's apartment building. "Okay. After we're done here, we'll check in with you at the hospital."

"Yeah, sounds like Ted could be there awhile. He suffered a few nasty blows to the head and kidneys."

Cole parked the ambulance next to the command post. He hoped by now they had tapped into the surveillance cameras. They hadn't all been blacked out, so one of the cameras at the exits should've caught the kids running. "How are you doing?" he called back to Sherri, glancing in the rearview mirror.

She held an icepack against her nose. "Dan doesn't think it's broken."

"That's a relief." Cole climbed into the back with them.

"I'm more concerned about internals." Serious concern shadowed Dan's eyes. "The girl in the group was vicious, stomped on her abdomen."

Cole's blood pressure rocketed back through the roof. "Should we go straight to the hospital?" He searched Sherri's eyes. "I don't want to jeopardize your health."

She smiled her appreciation. "I'm tender and bruised, but I think that's the extent of it. I'll feel better if I can take care of the IDs now."

"Okay." Cole didn't hesitate to wrap an arm around her waist to help her out of the back of the ambulance and into the massive truck they used as a mobile command post.

She leaned into his side and whispered, "Thank you for finding us. I knew you would." At her unreserved confidence, his heart swelled. He wasn't sure he deserved it, but it felt amazing.

The technician sat in front of a blank security monitor "Afraid we have no video record of the attack. But…" The technician pressed the rewind button for the blacked-out screen of the food court camera and hit pause when an image appeared. "We got a pic of the perpetrator."

The image of a kid holding up a spray can, his face obscured by a ball cap, filled the screen.

"His timing couldn't have been better," the technician observed. "Security officers were too busy responding to the emergency to pay attention to the monitors."

"You've got nothing on him before this? Walking toward the camera?" Cole asked.

"Nope." The technician rewound the feed in slow motion. "The kid knew what he was doing. See that? He ducked in from underneath the camera."

"I don't recognize the ball cap," Sherri said. "Have you looked at the feed on the north entrance? They ran that way after everyone else had evacuated."

The tech pulled up that camera's feed and slowly rewound it.

"There!" Sherri pointed to a group of kids on the screen. "That's got to be them. Three guys and a girl and another kid with a backpack. I forgot about him. He was yelling at them to hurry up."

"He looks like he could be our spray painter."

The tech backed up the feed to where the group first appeared mere seconds after the last of the crowd of shoppers disappeared out the exit. "They never look at the camera. It's going to be next to impossible to get an ID on them. If they're all minors we won't be able to televise this on the evening news."

"Is there a camera between this view and the food court?"

"No. That's all we got."

Cole hated the deflated look that crossed Sherri's face. "Don't worry. There are lots more here than it seems. Three of the guys are wearing high tops and the girl's shoes look unique. I want you to pull every detail you can off these tapes and get deputies on the pavement checking news cameras and anyone else who might've filmed people pouring out of that entrance. Someone had to get a picture of their faces."

Sherri began to describe one of the kids in minute detail, right down to his pug nose and icy-blue eyes.

The sheriff stepped into the command post. "We just got word that a couple of teens cleaned out shelves of painkillers and cold medicine in the pharmacy in the confusion."

"Any narcotics taken?"

"No. Thankfully, the pharmacist caged the good drugs before evacuating." The sheriff ran his finger down the list of cameras mall security provided. "Pull up camera twelve."

The tech brought it up on the screen and paused the rewinding feed when the looters appeared.

"You recognize those two?" the sheriff asked Sherri.

"No. I never saw them."

The sheriff clucked. "Okay, the two incidents might not be connected. These boys could just be opportunists. The others obviously had put a lot of planning into the attack."

"Seems like overkill for what few narcotics they'd have pulled out of our trauma bag," Dan spoke up. "Even the morphine vials probably don't have a street value of much more than ten bucks each."

The sheriff nodded and focused on Sherri. "That's why we're assuming *you* were the target."

Sherri blanched as if the idea hadn't occurred to her. She spun toward Dan, apology filling her eyes. "This is my fault."

Cole wrapped an arm around her shoulder, curling it until she was snug against his chest. He ignored the sheriff's narrowed gaze. If he fired him for inappropriate conduct, it was a price he'd willingly pay if it meant making this day a fraction easier on Sherri.

"This isn't your fault," he said softly.

But there was no doubt she had been the target.

* * *

"I don't know, Cole." She crawled into the back of the ambulance and hugged her knees. "I thought being a paramedic was what God wanted me to do. Why He let me live. Why Luke made me promise not to quit." She rocked herself back and forth, but she couldn't stop herself. "I…I forced myself to shut out the fears. To shrug off the pranks to prove I wouldn't let them stop me from helping people the way God wanted." She swiped at her running nose, blinked back the sting of tears. "Only now other people are getting hurt and I don't know what I'm supposed to do."

Cole hunkered down beside her on the floor of the ambulance and wrapped her in his arms. "Oh, sweetheart, it seems to me the gift Luke saw in you was being yourself, a person who cares deeply for others. A person who is more concerned about allaying the fears of a frightened child than being hit by sparks from the firefighters working to free her legs. Your empathy is your gift." He lifted her chin and looked at her as though he really believed what he was saying. As though he really believed in her. "I never forgot how sweetly you treated my hand and listened to my woes the day I learned my parents were divorcing."

"But I can't let myself *feel*, and do my job. It's too overwhelming." She shook her head. "Not that it'll matter anymore. They'll probably never let me come back to work."

"Why? Because a stalker is targeting you?"

"Because…" The tears started to fall. She swiped at her eyes, blinked to try and stop them. But she couldn't. *She couldn't.* "Because I can't pretend I'm not falling apart anymore!"

He tucked her head under his chin, and his husky voice rumbled through her. "No matter how noble your reasons for hiding your emotions, I don't think that's what God ever intended. Remember what He told the Apostle Paul? His power is made perfect in weakness." Cole laid his cheek against the top of her head, but his comforting touch, his sweet words made her cry all the more.

"Shh," Cole soothed. "You've been afraid to show your weakness, but God wants to be your strength." He tightened his hold. "Sometimes the greatest gift you can give to someone is to let them see your vulnerability."

She drew in a ragged breath.

Cole stroked her back comfortingly. "Your family, your friends, your colleagues would all want to help you…if you'd let them in."

She shook her head. "People shy away from messed-up people. They don't want to be burdened. My parents would just coddle me and wrap me in cotton batting if they could, but the rest of the family wouldn't understand. They're all cops and firefighters, and none of them have trouble coping with the job. I'd be a disappointment to the Steele name."

Cole actually had the nerve to chuckle. Here she was baring her soul to him and he was laughing at her! She tried to pull out of his arms, but he refused to give ground. "Trust me, Sherri. We don't cope as well as you think. That's why too many officers drink too much or end up divorced. The ones who talk about whatever's eating at them and get support fare much better. I suspect your relatives fall into that category, because they have each other. Have you ever asked your cousin Jake if he had nightmares after losing his wife?"

"I couldn't do that." She pushed away from him. "Dredge up old grief. He has a new wife now."

"Yeah, and she's pregnant, and he lost his first wife soon after childbirth. Don't you think that might be preying on his mind?"

She gulped. "Okay, I get it. I know I'm not the only one with problems. But Jake certainly doesn't need to worry about my problems on top of his own."

"But don't you see?" Her heart melted at the earnestness in his gaze, the tenderness in his voice. "He does anyway. Because that's what families do—share each other's burdens. It's what God wants us to do."

His *I'm making it my problem* declaration his first day on the job, whispered through her mind. Did he consider her family?

The sheriff appeared at the back of the truck and held up a baggie containing a key ring. "These belong to you?"

"Yes." Sherri stepped away from Cole and stuffed the keys in her pocket. "They must have fallen out when that creep searched me for drugs. Thank goodness he didn't take them." She shivered at the thought of her attackers waiting for her in her apartment.

"We haven't found any more bombs," the sheriff told Cole, his tone short. "But we found fingerprints on the one that didn't detonate that might give us a lead. I've sent a deputy over to Joe Martello's to bring him in for questioning."

"What?" Dan stepped up beside the sheriff and turned a disgusted glare her way. "You think Joe did this to you?"

Sherri slanted a panicked glance at Cole. She'd specifically begged him to make sure Joe wouldn't know.

"No, *I* think he did," Cole said. "He's the only suspect with substantial motive."

Dan snorted. "You don't know him at all. He's turned his life around thanks to Sherri snitching on him. He's not going to throw that all away. For what? Revenge?" Dan waved off Cole's attempt to argue. "Forget it. Let's get Sherri to the hospital, and then I got to get the ambulance restocked for the next shift."

Sherri tensed at the thought of what else Dan was likely in a hurry to do—talk to Joe. Whether he was behind the attacks or not, finding out they suspected him would only make him mad and make everything ten times worse.

TWELVE

Cole accompanied Sherri to the hospital to ensure whoever was after her didn't get to her there.

Two hours later, the ER doc gave her permission to go home, confirming that she'd suffered no serious internal injuries. "But you'll have someone with you?"

"Yes," she conceded, slanting Cole a sheepish glance, since it had taken a bit of arm-twisting to convince her to stay at her parents'. Of course, given her condition, Cole wouldn't be surprised if her father locked her in for good.

Cole escorted her to where Zeke was keeping an eye out for the deputy dropping off their cruiser, since they'd both ridden to the hospital in ambulances. "How are you really doing?" he whispered close to her ear. Between doctor exams and tests and his keeping tabs on the investigation status, they hadn't had another opportunity to talk. He'd noticed the mask slip back into place as soon as Dan had given him an earful about their suspicions of Joe.

"Better. I'm going to think about what you said. Is Ted okay? I want to thank him for coming to my rescue again."

"That will have to wait. They're keeping him in for observation. But—" Cole produced a key from his pocket "—he was so eager to help us identify your attackers that he handed over his house key so I can peruse the photos he took of you."

She jolted to an abrupt stop. "He took pictures of me?"

Cole grimaced. "That's what he said. And to be honest, I have no idea how creepy that really is until I see them. He figures we might see some familiar faces in the background."

"Then I should come." She squared her shoulders and jutted her chin, looking ready to argue if he said no.

Zeke joined them. "Sounds like a good idea. C'mon, our ride's here."

Cole reluctantly conceded that it would be expedient to let her come along.

Ted's second-story apartment was only two blocks from Sherri's, but in a markedly more financially depressed neighborhood. Noisy air conditioners dangled precariously from every third window in the building. There was no front-door security, and the stairwells reeked of stale beer. The arrival of a sheriff's car wouldn't surprise anyone here.

In contrast, the man's apartment was neat and pleasant smelling.

"I feel as if we're invading his privacy coming in without him," Sherri whispered, not straying far from the front door.

"Get over it." Zeke strutted in like he owned the place. "He said we could. Insisted he didn't think we should wait until he was out of the hospital." Zeke made a beeline down the hall, glancing in each room as he went. Ted had said his pictures were in the second bedroom, which he used as an office, some printed, some only on his computer.

"Whoa." Zeke paused outside the room and shot Cole a maybe-you-don't-want-to-bring-her-in-here look.

"What is it?" Sherri asked.

"Wait here a sec." Cole hurried to Zeke's side and all but choked at the hundreds of photographs of Sherri that papered the wall—a whole lot more than ten days' worth. "The guy's obsessed with her," Cole whispered. He'd already known it in his gut, but he hadn't had a clue just *how* obsessed.

"Downright certifiable, I'd say."

Cole stepped fully into the room and studied

the photos. Ones of her leaving the ambulance base. Ones of her going into the coffee shop. Except they looked like they could date back a couple of years—coming out of the movie theater, out of church, out jogging on the river trail. Then there were time-stamped ones, more recent. Ones of Sherri working calls, others off duty. Each picture captured other people in the background and the odd person who appeared to be watching her. Cole sucked in a sharp breath. Unfortunately, in at least three, that odd person was his brother, Eddie.

Sherri's gasp snapped Cole's attention back to the bedroom door. She stood on the threshold, ashen and trembling.

He rushed to her and clasped her shoulders, forcing her gaze to meet his.

"He's, he's…crazy."

"About you, it seems," Cole added solemnly. "Do you know why?"

"How am I supposed to know?" Her voice rose hysterically. "I've never seen him before he saved me from that dog, but…but…" She walked into the room and studied the pictures, wrapping her arms around herself as if she'd been plunged into a snowstorm. "Clearly, he's been watching me for a lot longer than that."

"Yeah—" Zeke lifted a lock of hair from a shrinelike table beneath the wall of photos and held it close to hers "—a real nut job. My guess is that his rescues were no coincidence. He's probably been setting you up just so he can play your hero."

She swung her head away from the lock of hair in Zeke's hand. "That's crazy."

"Yeah." Zeke motioned to the wall and let out a snort. "That's what he is."

Sherri's legs wobbled and her arms quivered. She almost looked in worse shape than when he'd found her in the food court. Then she'd been able to fight, but this was too personal, too insidious.

Cole eased her into a chair. "His obsession didn't come out of thin air. You saved his life three years ago. Do you remember?"

"No! And how do *you* know if I don't remember?"

"We saw him talking to his former neighbor when we were following him earlier and after he left, we asked her about him." Cole reminded Sherri about the call and how she'd revived him. "He was apparently a lot thinner then, which would explain why you didn't recognize him."

"Yes. I think I do remember him now. I was scared out of my wits because I'd never used the defibrillator solo on a real patient before. After I revived him, he looked at me so oddly. It was dark and we were outside. Joe said he probably saw the headlights beaming through my hair."

"Well, apparently, he's made it his mission to look out for you."

Sherri relaxed a little. "That's kind of sweet."

"If it weren't so creepy," Zeke interjected, snapping photos of the montage.

Sherri shuddered. "Yeah."

"I'd say we've got enough here to hold him on a psych evaluation until we can prove he set up all the stunts to play her hero." Zeke plopped into the desk chair and flicked on the computer. "We might even find his plans on here."

"He only gave us permission to look at the photos," Cole reminded him, not wanting to sabotage a conviction by acquiring evidence without a warrant. Not that he was quite ready to believe Ted was behind everything. How did a mall custodian win the cooperation of so many teenagers?

Okay, maybe that wasn't so hard to believe. He could've promised to sneak them into the movie theater the back way or given them tips on how to beat mall security for their own exploits. But how'd he convince some Rottweiler owner to sic his dog on Sherri? Let alone know when she'd be the one to respond to a 9-1-1 call?

Of course, who was to say there hadn't been other calls that he'd opted not to exploit because another team had responded those times?

"Jackpot." Zeke motioned them over to the computer. "Look at these."

The screen had thumbnails of more than fifty photos.

Sherri squinted at the screen and shivered. "This was yesterday. I had a feeling someone was watching me."

Cole fisted his hand. He'd been watching her while on his patrols yesterday, too. But clearly not closely enough.

Zeke clicked on Slideshow and, one at a time, the photos filled the screen. Ones of Sherri walking downtown with Jake's wife, coming out of the bakery with her, talking to her outside the fire station, talking with Cole outside the sheriff's office. "Look—" Zeke pointed to the bench in front of the sheriff's office "—he even caught me watching you in that one."

Two more photos of their argument followed in quick succession, each from different angles. "Stop on that one," Cole said. "Isn't that Joe watching from outside the ambulance base with Dan?"

"Yeah, he'd been paying the guys a visit. He was already there when I stopped by. He couldn't have known I'd show up, because I hadn't planned to. But I'm not surprised they stepped outside to watch the show after the way I stormed out."

Cole took consolation in the self-denigration

in her voice as she looked back at their argument now. "In the interest of full disclosure, you should know that Eddie was at the mall at the time of the 9-1-1 call and subsequent bomb threat."

Her eyes widened, then searched his. Her expression morphed from surprised to unreadable. "Do you think he was involved?"

"He claimed he was hanging with friends. I'll have to trace his movements back through every video feed that picked him up to decide if it's the truth. I'll also show him the stills of the five teens leaving the mall. Ask if he can identify them. Gauge his reaction."

Zeke shook his head. "You'd better let me do that. Your judgment's tainted."

Cole restrained a frustrated sigh. He was probably right, but Cole didn't like the gleam that crept into Zeke's eyes or the way his lips edged up as if it would be a pleasure to prove how tainted.

"We already know he's friends with Ted," Zeke stated.

"Eddie is friends with him?" Fresh outrage simmered in Sherri's voice, as if she thought this was yet something else they'd kept from her.

Cole scowled at Zeke. "I don't know anything of the kind. How do you figure?"

"After the dog attack, when you and Eddie came out of the woods, he caught a ride into town with Ted."

"Eddie stuck out his thumb, and Ted picked him up." Cole didn't bother to hide his irritation with Zeke for reading more into the scenario.

"Or so he'd like you to *believe…*"

"I'm not crazy!" Ted yelled as Cole supervised his transfer to the psych ward. "There's no law against taking pictures, is there? If she doesn't want me taking pictures I'll stop. I swear I will."

"I'm sure she'd appreciate that," Cole said.

As the orderly wheeled Ted into a secure room, he grabbed Cole's hand. "You don't believe I'd hurt her, do you? She saved my life. I'd never hurt her. I was watching out for her."

Not at liberty to question him without his lawyer present, Cole restricted his response to a nod and pried his hand free of Ted's grip.

"It's that other deputy you should be investigating. He's the crazy one, thinking I'd sic a dog on Sherri just so I could rescue her. What took him so long to get to the scene, huh?" Ted scratched his fingers up and down the arm of the wheelchair. "I heard the call on my police band at home. Heard him respond right away, too. Said he was on his way. But I still got there before him. Why's that, huh?" Ted grew more agitated, rocking in his chair. "Did he tell you I asked him that when he questioned me after the attack?"

Cole hid his shock. Not surprised that his partner had neglected to mention being quizzed about his slow response time, but that he hadn't clued in to the oddity himself. He'd been at the coffee shop across the street when Zeke phoned to report the 9-1-1 call. There was no way he should've beat Zeke to the scene, let alone by more than a five-minute margin.

"I didn't think so," Ted went on. "He's a slimy one, that one. You can see it in his eyes. Sure, I know some about dogs. Enough to know Sherri's partner was an idiot to tell her to make eye contact and hold out her hand. But what does he think? I'm a ventriloquist and threw a whistle out to those woods to get the dog to run off? I'm telling you, he's the nutcase."

"I assure you we'll conduct a thorough investigation and appreciate your cooperation." Cole left Ted to the psychiatrist's care and headed back to the station. Rationally, he knew the man was lashing out, looking for someone else to blame, but Cole wasn't ready to overlook Zeke's slow response time to the dog attack, either.

As Cole pulled into the office parking lot, Zeke barreled out of the building. "You're here. Good. We just got IDs on two of the teens in the video surveillance from one of the high school teachers. They live in a foster home out on Fifth. We need to hurry if we're going to catch them before they leave for school."

"Hop in." Cole flipped on the sirens and careened out of the lot.

"You might want to kill the sirens before we get to Fifth," Zeke suggested. "If they think we're coming for them, they might make a run for it."

Deciding the kids probably already had started walking to school if they didn't intend to ditch classes, Cole cut the sirens and headed to Fifth from the direction of the school.

"There they are!" Zeke pointed to three teens— two males and a female—who took off the other way the instant they spotted the cruiser.

Cole whipped the car past them and ramped onto the curb. Before he'd rammed the shifter into Park, Zeke's door flew open. "They're getting away!"

The threesome cut across a yard.

Cole called for backup and sprinted for the next lot to try to cut them off. He hit the next street, two strides ahead of Zeke and three behind the slowest kid. The kid's baggy pants slid farther down his backside, tangling with his unlaced court shoes, tripping him up. Cole snagged the back of the shorter kid's shirt before he face planted the sidewalk. Zeke puffed after the second male and, catching him by the coat, slammed his face into the yard's chain-link fence.

"We didn't do nothin'." Zeke's five-foot-six, jock-type kid griped, fighting against Zeke's hold.

Zeke wrenched the kid's arm higher up his back. "Sure, that's why you ran." He patted down the kid more roughly than necessary and hissed who knows what kind of warnings in his ear as he turned the kid's pockets inside out.

Cole directed his quaking kid to hold his hands against the fence. He looked too young to fit Sherri's description of the suspects in the mall attack. He'd wet his pants, and Cole almost felt sorry for him…until Cole's fingers closed around a vial in the kid's pocket. A morphine vial.

Cole held the vial in front of the kid's face—a face that looked too much like his brother's I-just-want-the-kids-to-like-me look of not so many years ago. If only he'd recognized the signs then, he might've stopped Eddie's downward spiral. "Where'd you get this?"

The boy pressed his lips into a tight line and dropped his gaze to the dirt. No snitch.

"This kid sell it to you?" Zeke seethed, shoving his suspect toward Cole's.

The boy vigorously shook his head, his gaze not lifting past his friend's chest. Although Cole suspected the kid was no friend. Cole gentled his voice. "What's your name?"

"Jimmy. Jimmy Myers," he said, his voice no louder than a mouse's squeak.

Zeke snorted in disgust and gave his suspect a shake. "Don't think a snot-nosed kid's testimony is gonna save you this time. We got you on tape." Zeke kicked the kid's foot. "Right down to those fancy shoes."

Two more cruisers pulled up, one with the girl who'd outrun them already socked in the backseat. Three of the four deputies stepped out of their cars. "We can take in this lot if you want to pick up their foster mother. Save you dragging them back to your car."

Zeke handed his suspect off to the deputy and had a few words with the girl in their backseat.

"He didn't sell me the vial," Jimmy said, loud enough for the other kid to hear, no doubt a last-ditch effort to keep a shred of dignity. Was that what Eddie's denial had been, too? Did he really still care what Cole thought of him? Cole hoped so, because then he might have a fighting chance of turning him around.

Zeke returned to Jimmy and got in his face. "You're not doing him or that girl any favors by covering for them, you know. He doesn't care about you or that girl. He's going to get her addicted, and three years from now she'll be turning tricks to pay for her next high. What if that was your little sister?" He shoved the white-faced kid into the back of the second cruiser. "Do you want that on your conscience?"

"Take it easy," Cole said after Zeke shut the door. "That's a lot to put on a kid."

Zeke drilled Cole with a scowl so vehement the whites of his eyes flamed red. "Maybe if you'd put it on your kid brother, he wouldn't be such a mess up. Ever think of that?"

Cole blew out a breath. Yeah. Every hour of every day.

THIRTEEN

Sherri strained to slow her choppy breathing at the sight of Dan exiting the room across the corridor from the sheriff's office. "Is it them?" she asked him as he passed.

Cole silenced him with a raised hand before Dan could respond. "You need to decide for yourself. There are more teens in the lineup than our suspects. We need you to identify the ones who attacked you." Cole escorted her into the tiny dark room.

Catching sight of the lineup of teen boys on the other side of the glass, she said, "They can't see me, can they?"

"No," Cole reassured. "Take your time."

"Number two. I recognize those eyes and pug nose and that scar on his lip." She scanned the faces of three and four and gasped when she reached the one on the end. "What's Eddie doing in the lineup? He didn't attack us. I would have told you."

Cole glanced past her shoulder.

She spun on her heel as a deputy stepped out of the shadows. "He fit the age and description and was at the mall at the time of the incident. We needed to make sure."

"I understand, of course."

Next they brought in a line of five teen girls. Sherri studied each in turn and as she shifted her gaze to number five her heart jolted. The girl seemed to be looking right at her. Reflexively, she pressed her palm to her abdomen, remembering how viciously the girl had stomped on it. "Number five," she said, hating how her voice cracked.

Cole squeezed her shoulder. "You okay?"

She nodded without meeting his gaze, not sure she could hold herself together if she saw the compassion she knew would be there. She didn't know why God was allowing all these bad things to happen to her, but she thanked Him every day for bringing Cole back into her life to help her through.

"We appreciate your coming in, Miss Steele," the other deputy cut in. "We know this must be difficult for you. If you could spare us a few more minutes, we have collected some high school yearbooks and mug shots we'd like you to look through to see if you can identify any of the other assailants."

"Yes. I'll do whatever you need me to do."

Cole led her to a conference room, empty save for the stack of yearbooks sitting in the middle of a long table. He pulled out a chair for her. "Can I get you a cup of coffee? Tea?"

The reserve in his voice, the stiffness of his movements bothered her more than it should have. This was his work. No matter how much he might care about her, he needed to treat her as the witness and victim she was, or they'd probably pull him off the case altogether. She sat down and pulled the top book from the stack. "A glass of water would be nice. Thanks."

He slipped out, closing the door behind him.

Two books later she rubbed the grit from her eyes as he returned empty-handed. His hair poked every which way as if he'd been raking his fingers through it. "Out of water?" she asked with a hint of amusement.

"Oh." He started back out.

"No, no, it's okay. Tell me what's going on."

He walked to the window and gazed outside, even though there was nothing to see but a brick wall. "The two kids you IDed confessed."

"That's great."

His expression looked pained.

"It's not great?"

"I'm not sure." Cole straddled the chair at the end of the table. "They claim they don't know who the other three were and both fingered a mall custodian as the guy who put them up to it."

"Ted?"

"We showed each of them a selection of staff photos and he is who they both pointed to, yes."

"So what's bothering you?"

"It's too neat. They claim Ted supplied them with the smoke bombs and the spray paint to black out the security cameras."

"Seems believable to me. A guy who works in a mall day in and day out is bound to be able to figure out how to avoid security if he's paying attention."

"Sure, but we can't find any evidence that Ted made any such purchases or built the smoke bombs."

"So it's their word against his."

"Basically, and the photos of you in his apartment don't help his case any."

Sherri splayed her fingers on the tabletop. "Well, I've got to admit that having someone obsessed with the desire to be my hero is easier to stomach than the thought of Joe or Luke's father or who knows who wanting to terrorize me. Don't you think?"

He gave a one-shouldered shrug, not looking too convinced.

"Why aren't you happier about this? With Ted

locked up in the psych ward and half his minions off the street, I should be safe now, right?"

Cole reached across the table and covered her hand. "I want to believe that, Sherri, but I don't like what my gut is telling me."

"What's it telling you?"

Cole glanced at his watch. "Did you have any luck with the books?"

She blinked, thrown by his avoidance of the question. "Not yet. I only got through two."

"We can take the rest with us. Let's go." He scooped up the remaining books and opened the door. "Give me a sec." He popped his head into the sheriff's office. "I'm driving Miss Steele home. She's taking the rest of the books to look at." He prodded her down the corridor toward the back door.

"Cole, what's going on? I don't mind looking at the rest of those here."

"We can't talk here," Cole whispered. Instead of steering her toward the cruiser he'd picked her up in two hours ago, he steered her to his truck. "Are your folks home?"

"My mom is. Why?"

"I'd rather not talk where we could be over-heard." Cole backed out of his parking spot and headed south, his gaze straying to his mirrors every few seconds.

"Where are we going?"

"Here." He turned into the parking lot next to the trailhead for the river trail they'd been jogging every morning. He shut off the engine and when he turned toward her, hitching his knee onto the seat between them, his expression looked pained. "I'm afraid that I'm the reason all these bad things have been happening to you."

"What? Why? That's ridiculous."

"Hear me out." The ache in his voice made her heart twist. "Remember my theory that Joe, or whoever had been setting you up, got scared when I started investigating, and framed Eddie to derail my investigation?"

"Yes."

"I think it was Zeke and his nephew framing him."

"Zeke? But all kinds of things happened to me before you came back to town."

"Yes, and maybe someone else is behind those, or maybe you were right and you'd had a run of being the dark cloud. Either way, after you caught Eddie in your ambulance, I think Zeke and his nephew saw the potential to exploit Eddie's condition to make me look bad or to goad me into doing something corrupt to protect him."

"But why would they do that?"

"I got the opening Zeke's nephew was after for one. Then there's a bunch of little things like why'd Zeke show up five minutes after me at the dog attack when he'd told me he was on his way when he called me? And since I was still off duty with the concussion, I left him to visit all the Rottweiler owners except Luke's father." He dug his clenched fist into his thigh. "For all I know, he covered up for the owner. Said the dog was there when it wasn't. I can go back and check every one myself. But if any are missing a dog now, they could say it only just went missing."

"But Zeke's a deputy sheriff." She trailed her fingers over his clenched ones, hoping to soothe his tension. "Do you really think he'd jeopardize my life to get you kicked off the force so his nephew could apply for a position he still might not get?"

"I know it seems crazy." He turned his hand beneath hers and gently clasped her fingers. "I hate to think that my being here has in any way endangered you, but Zeke was in a position to know when your ambulance was the only one at the base and would be the next to be dispatched. Either he or his nephew could've pretended to be Eddie's drug pusher and called to lure him to the drug house, then phoned 9-1-1 from the pay phone."

"But those kids. They said Ted bribed them to attack me and Dan."

"When Zeke and I made the arrests, he whispered something to each of the kids. I thought he was trying to put the fear of God into them, but now I think he might have been cuing them to finger Ted."

"Are you serious?"

Cole winced. "You've got to admit that Zeke seemed pretty eager to arrest Ted. I don't think that had been his original plan. He probably hoped to nail Eddie, but the surveillance tapes cleared him, and Ted's being in the food court when we showed up made him a convenient scapegoat."

"How does Zeke's nephew fit into all this?"

"That's what I only just figured out, thanks to a comment made by the deputy that Zeke handed the mall staff photographs to." Cole pulled a photo from his back pocket. "Do you recognize this guy?"

"Yeah, he's the security guard who directed us to the food court and then disappeared."

"He's also Zeke's nephew."

Her heart jumped. "Oh, wow." She stared at the photograph. "Oh. Wow."

"Yeah. Planting the smoke bombs would've been easy for him, as well as giving the teens tips on how to avoid the cameras. He was also the one who met us in the security room. I should have clued in the second he stammered over your location in the mall."

"But…" She swallowed. "That girl's kicks could have killed me. How far will Zeke and his nephew go to get what they want?" She pictured Zeke in his deputy's uniform, thought about the power he wielded. "How can we stop them?"

Cole spent most of the next day at his desk working on reports and cross-referencing data from all the incidents involving Sherri. With Ted positioned to take the fall, he was confident Zeke wouldn't risk pulling any more stunts. But verifying he'd been behind the others wasn't proving to be easy, even with Zeke tied up in court all day and not around to look over his shoulder.

Of course, being preoccupied with thoughts of Sherri and the dinner she'd agreed to share with him tonight wasn't helping. *Speaking of which...* Cole glanced at his watch and closed his files. He didn't want to keep her waiting.

At his request she'd moved back in with her parents for the time being. A strange feeling pinched his gut as he turned on to the street that had been his for the first eighteen years of his life. At the sight of his dad and Eddie talking to Sherri over the fence between their childhood homes, Cole fought the urge to step on the gas. He parked at the curb and sat there, watching their easy conservation, an odd longing to be part of it warring with the feeling that he'd be betraying his mother if he joined in.

His heart twisted. He was probably an idiot for

asking Sherri out in the first place. She might be feeling grateful right now for his concern about her, but once her life settled back down, he'd still be the brother of the drug addict who'd assaulted her and the son of a man who'd cheated on his wife. Not prime long-term relationship material. Never mind that his being here likely had been what had triggered all her troubles in the first place.

Well, maybe not all her troubles.

He closed his eyes, remembering how she'd burrowed into his chest and cried her eyes out as they'd stood beside her partner's grave. Everything in him longed to take away her pain. At the same time, he feared he'd only end up causing her more. He lifted his gaze.

Dad offered him an uncertain smile and a small wave.

Cole nodded and, prying three fingers from the truck's steering wheel, fluttered them in response. He should go over there and talk to him. Except his legs refused to cooperate.

A heartbeat later, Dad said something else to Sherri, reached across the fence and squeezed her hand, and then headed into the house without another glance Cole's way. Yeah, typical. Clearly he wasn't any more eager to move toward reconciliation than Cole was. In his mixed-up, immature eighteen-year-old mind, he'd figured staying away would be punishment, but he wasn't so sure Dad had cared. Sure, he'd sent a card for college graduation and said he'd have liked to be there.

Cole braced for the bitterness that usually piggybacked that thought. Surprisingly, it never came, only a pervasive sadness. That's one prayer God had answered anyway. "Thank you," he murmured. *Now, if You could help me get Eddie back on track, that would be great.*

Cole shoved open his truck door and sauntered to Sherri and Eddie.

"Hey." Eddie actually made eye contact, despite the fact that their last conversation had consisted of Cole interrogating him over what he'd been doing at the mall and whether he could identify any of the punks who'd attacked Sherri. "Sherri says you caught the kids that hurt her."

"Some of them anyway." Cole squinted at him, trying to decide if Eddie's cheery disposition was the effect of a drug high or if God was already answering another prayer. They'd made plans to go to a ball game together on Saturday. It was a start.

"I wish I could've been more help."

Sherri clasped Eddie's arm. "Just stay away from guys like the one who sent you to my ambulance and we'll all be okay."

Eddie's cheeks flamed, his gaze dropping to her hand. "I will."

"Hey," Cole said, "would you like to join Sherri

and me for dinner? We might go mini-golfing afterward or maybe take in a movie."

"Nah. Dad's barbecuing steaks."

"Ah, can't compete with that." Nobody barbecued steaks as good as Dad. "We'll see you later, then." Cole caught Sherri's hand. "You ready to go?"

Two hours later Sherri's eyes twinkled with scarcely contained amusement as he missed yet another gimme putt on the final hole of their game.

Truth be told, he'd miss a thousand putts if it meant seeing her look so relaxed, happy and carefree. Not that he'd missed the putts on purpose. He shook his head, then reining in the smile tugging at his lips, tapped the ball into the hole for a double bogey. "This is your fault, you know. You're way too distracting."

Her eyes widened. "I'm distracting? I stood perfectly still and quiet while you putted. You're the one who cracked jokes trying to distract me, and when that didn't work you nudged the windmill to ricochet my golf ball back to the tee."

He laughed. "I had to do something to even the playing field. How was I supposed to keep my eye on the ball when you were standing there looking so beautiful?"

She blushed. "Now who's trying to distract who?"

Cole leaned on his putter and studied her,

knowing he was playing with fire but unable to come up with a single reason to stop as he watched joy bubble from her like a sparkling fountain.

"I'm beginning to think you asked your brother to join us so you wouldn't look so bad at the game," she teased.

"No—" all at once, he could think of nothing except kissing her. He caught her about the waist "—that was to keep me from doing this." He curled his arm to draw her to him. Her delicate scent invaded his senses, as it had been doing all night. Her lips shimmered in the spotlight shining down on them as he paused long enough for her to pull back. Her disarming smile touched a part of him he'd thought beyond reach and sent his already pounding heart thundering as their lips met.

She tasted of peppermint and chocolate, only sweeter. Much sweeter. She swayed toward him and joy and an intense possessiveness surged through him. Wrapping his arms around her, he drew her closer to deepen the kiss, only to be foiled by the blast of his phone. He managed to ignore it for two rings, until Sherri pulled back, a shy smile dancing on her lips.

"Aren't you going to answer that?"

He let out his best reluctantly acquiescent groan as he tugged the phone from his belt. "Hello."

"Cole?"

The anxiety in his dad's voice stripped the grin from Cole's lips. "What's wrong?" He dropped his hand to Sherri's, clutching it like a lifeline as a horrible premonition rampaged through his mind. His dad hadn't called him in seven years. Not once.

"Eddie's gone."

"What do you mean *gone*?" Cole demanded.

"I'll meet you at the truck," Sherri whispered and hurried over to the kiosk with their putters and golf balls.

"I took him to the video store on Canyon to pick out a couple of movies while I ran into the grocery store. But when I got back, he was gone."

Cole slowed his frantic stride and waited for Sherri to catch up. "Maybe he went looking for you at the grocery store."

"That's what I figured, because the video store had closed by the time I got back to it, but I went up and down every aisle in the grocery store and even tried having him paged. I can't find him."

"Have you tried his new phone?"

"He's not answering. I would have driven home to see if he started walking, but I didn't want him to find the car gone if he'd wandered off with a friend and came back. I've spent the last forty-five minutes searching every shop and corner of the parking lot."

"Forty-five minutes!" Cole opened the truck door for Sherri. "Okay, we're on our way."

"I tried calling the sheriff, but they said he had to be missing twenty-four hours—"

"I'll call. Was he still wearing the same clothes I saw him in?"

"And a navy blue windbreaker."

"I'll make sure the deputies are on the lookout for him. Hold tight. We'll be there in a few minutes." Cole hit Disconnect and tossed the phone to Sherri. "Dial the sheriff's direct line. He's in Contacts." He rammed the truck into Drive and squealed out of the parking lot.

An instant later Sherri filled the sheriff in on the reason for the call and handed the phone back to Cole. "Yeah, sheriff. I need a BOLO on Eddie."

"Your father already—"

"No, listen, sir, please. His sneaking off doesn't add up. Not tonight."

"He's done it before. Addicts can't quit as easily as they'd like us to think."

"Yeah, that's why we need every deputy on the lookout for him."

The sheriff's sigh told Cole that his boss had to be regretting ever hiring him. "I'm sorry, Cole. We just got word of an infant being kidnapped from his home. If not for your father's call, I would've already called you to come in. We've put out an Amber Alert and notified State Police, but I need every available deputy on this. I can put out the BOLO, but that's all I can do."

"We'll find him," Sherri said, taking back the phone.

Cole wanted to believe her, but the burn in his gut said something was very wrong. "Eddie was happy. Had a fun night planned with Dad. Dad can be a lot of fun to hang out with when he wants to be. I can't see Eddie ditching him."

Sherri reached across the seat and squeezed his hand. "We'll find him," she repeated.

Dad flagged them down the instant they pulled into the parking lot. "Did you talk to the sheriff?" he asked as Cole parked beside him and rolled down his window.

"Yes, but a baby's been kidnapped so they have more urgent priorities at the moment." Cole glanced in Dad's car and noted the single bag of groceries. "Is that all the groceries you picked up? What took you so long to get back to the video store?"

"A lady needed my help."

Right. Figured. He should've known.

"What do you think? Should I stick around here? It's getting dark. And he's more likely to remember the home number than my cell phone's if his phone's dead. And it's got to be." Dad turned his phone screen their way. "I bought him a phone I can track, but I'm not picking it up. See?"

Or Eddie had deliberately scuttled the feature. The burn in Cole's gut spread to his chest. The situation was looking worse by the second. "Okay, you head back to the house. Call his friends. Ask them all to be on the lookout for him. Keep trying his cell. Sherri and I will drive around and look for him."

"Maybe he caught up with a friend and lost track of time," Sherri suggested.

Yeah, but Cole doubted it, especially if he'd wandered to the grocery to see what had been taking Dad so long and spotted him flirting with another floozy. "Let's hope they're walking the street, then." He and Sherri trolled the area in ever-widening blocks.

When he neared Sherri's street, she said, "Why don't you let me off at my apartment and I can pick up my car? I wanted to bring it to my folks' tonight, anyway, and we'll be able to cover more ground that way."

Cole slapped his hand on the steering wheel. "Why can't my dad ignore women for one lousy night? Eddie would be home watching a movie with him if Dad hadn't wasted who knows how long *helping* some desperate woman."

"Your dad loves your brother and you. You need to forgive him. Holding on to your anger isn't helping Eddie."

Everything in him stiffened. "This is exactly

why I can't forgive him. The man cares only about himself." Cole twisted his fisted hands around the steering wheel. "I should've known this would happen. I shouldn't have gone out tonight."

Sherri glanced away.

"Hey." Feeling like a heel, Cole reached across the seat and gave her hair a gentle tug. "I don't regret going out with you." *Not really.* He traced the scar Eddie had left on her cheek. "Although why you'd want to get mixed up with me, I don't know." He returned his attention to the sidewalks, a sigh seeping from his chest. "You deserve a lot better."

She let out an unladylike snort. "You quit your job to pick up and move back to a town you never wanted to see again just so you could help your brother. And ever since you got here you haven't stopped looking out for me, too. What's not to appreciate?"

He shook his head. "You never cease to amaze me." He squeezed her hand. "But I'd rather you stick with me, tonight. If Eddie was mad at Dad, he could've gone drug seeking. After what he did to you the last time, I don't want you to find him without me." Cole drove past her apartment building.

"Cole, stop!" Sherri slammed her palm to his dash, her gaze fixed on his side window.

He rammed the brakes. "You see him?"

"There's someone in my car."

Cole hitched his arm over the back of his seat and reversed far enough to pull into her apartment parking lot. As his headlights swept over her windshield, his breath caught. Eddie was in the passenger seat. "He must've come here looking for me." Only Eddie was leaning against the window, his head flopped forward.

Sherri was already racing for her car, before Cole registered stopping his truck. She yanked on the door and when it didn't give, fumbled in her purse.

Cole raced to the driver's side. "It's locked, too!" He tried smashing the window with his elbow.

"I got the key," Sherri shouted, yanking open the door and catching Eddie as he tipped out. "Help me get him to the ground."

Cole hooked his arms under Eddie's and hauled him out. Under the harsh beams of Cole's headlights, Eddie's face looked deathly gray. "Is he breathing? He's not breathing!"

"Call 9-1-1." Sherri pressed an ear to Eddie's chest, then pounded it hard and started compressions. "C'mon, Eddie. Don't you die on me."

Cole punched the numbers. "I screwed up. I shouldn't have left him."

"What's your emergency?" the operator came

on and the words balled in Cole's throat, his gaze fixed on Eddie's lifeless face. "Hello?"

"My brother, he's not breathing. We need an ambulance."

"Your location?"

His mind drew a blank. "Sherri, what's the address?"

She shouted it out and Cole repeated it into the phone. The welcoming peal of sirens soon filled the air.

He dropped to his knees beside Sherri. "What can I do? Tell me what to do."

She continued pumping Eddie's chest hard and fast. "Call your dad." She looked up and his heart froze at the chill in her eyes.

"Oh, God, please—" The prayer died on his lips as he clutched his brother's hand. It was cold. Too cold.

FOURTEEN

The swirl of emergency lights in the darkness cast a sickly glow over Eddie's face. Sherri stepped back to give the arriving paramedic team room to take over. She'd gotten a pulse—weak, but there. Cole still clung to his brother's hand, willing him to live, and either ignoring or not hearing the paramedic's request that he step back.

She pried Cole's fingers from around Eddie's and pulled him away. "He's alive, Cole. You need to give them room to work. Okay?"

He turned to her, but seemed to look through her, unseeing.

"Cole, pull yourself together," she said sternly, hoping to snap him out of his shock.

"What did he take?" Jeff, the paramedic intubating asked.

A deputy backed out of her car, holding up a half-empty bottle. "Oxycontin and whiskey, by the looks of it."

That snapped Cole out of his daze. "No way.

My brother was not drinking tonight." Cole looked ready to pound the deputy for the mere suggestion.

Sherri tried to restrain him. "Cole, take it easy. He was drinking. I could smell it on his breath."

His tortured gaze broke her heart. "But…why? He'd been happy when we left."

The deputy made a notation on his notepad. "When a depressed person formulates a plan they think will fix their problems, they can often become unusually happy. That's when you really need to worry about them."

"What are you saying?" Cole lunged for the guy. "That my brother planned to kill himself?"

Sherri clasped his arms. "Cole, it's okay."

He flung off her hold. "It's not okay. My brother did not try to kill himself. He wouldn't."

She held her ground, understanding how desperately he'd want to believe that, but needing him to focus on what mattered most now. No matter how much it hurt. "Cole, what's important is he didn't succeed. You have another chance to be there for him. You need to focus on Eddie."

The deputy drew closer, a piece of paper and jackknife in his hand. "This your brother's knife?"

Cole took it and stroked the ivory inlay with his thumb. "Yeah. I gave it to him for his tenth birthday."

The deputy showed them the scrawled note

in his other hand. "It was used to pin this to the center of the steering wheel."

Sherri's knees buckled at the message: You win.

Was this meant for her? Did Eddie feel as if he was competing with her for his brother's attention? She'd had no idea.

"Do you know what he could have meant?" the deputy asked.

Cole's gaze met hers, his expression utterly tortured. Neither said a word, but she knew he was regretting pulling her deeper into his family's problems. Every time he looked at her now, what he'd remember was that he'd been with her when he should have been with his brother.

And he wouldn't be able to forgive himself. She'd replayed Luke's shooting in her mind enough times to know that.

She stiffened her spine, stuffed her trembling hands in her pockets and forced herself not to give in to the turmoil thrashing through her insides. She didn't know how Eddie had jimmied her door lock, but that effort alone had convinced her he'd chosen her car to make a statement. He'd resented Cole not being here all these years. That much had been obvious. It made sense, too, that he'd resent Cole spending so much time with her now that he was finally home.

Sherri felt for Eddie. He was hurting, but the

fact that he'd used the knife Cole had given him to pin this note to her car showed he'd clearly wanted to hurt Cole, too.

The paramedics loaded Eddie onto a gurney and into the back of the ambulance. "You riding to the hospital with us or following?"

"I need to go with him," Cole said to her, his tone vacant.

"Yes, you do."

"If you want to leave me your keys, we can drop your truck round to the hospital for you," the deputy said.

"Thank you." Cole handed over the keys.

Sherri stood and watched as the ambulance sped down the street, kept watching as the numbness seeped from her body and the trembling set in. She'd been afraid it would start before Cole left, escalating his guilt. She couldn't come between them. She wouldn't. Not again.

As the paramedic pushed open the back door of the ambulance, Cole spotted his dad waiting outside the ER doors and clenched his jaw to clamp down the fury threatening to explode out of him. The paramedics yanked out the gurney with Eddie's unconscious body, looking whiter than death, strapped on top. Dad stood frozen, his gaze fixed on the passing gurney, but making no move to check on his son.

Clambering from the truck, Cole diverted his attention back to Eddie.

Dad caught him by the shoulder as he passed. "How is he?"

"Alive, no thanks to you." Cole jerked free of his hold. If Dad had been giving Eddie the attention he craved, this wouldn't have happened.

They wheeled Eddie to a private room in the ER, and a nurse directed Cole to a waiting area. A few minutes later, Dad joined him with a clipboard full of forms. Cole fisted his hands and paced, wanting to lash out at him for letting this happen. But Dad's hollowed-out look gnawed at his insides, that and knowing he was as much to blame for Eddie's suicide attempt as his father. Maybe more. Eddie clearly resented how much time he spent with Sherri. He should've been home with him tonight, not with Sherri. Still...

"You couldn't have ignored women for one night?" Cole ranted. "Eddie probably went looking for you after the video store closed and saw you flirting with some floozy half your age."

Dad didn't look up from the paperwork he was filling out, but his fingers turned white where they gripped the pen. "Not everything is always what it seems."

"Clearly. You say you would've loved to come to my graduation. Yet, you didn't. As if anyone was stopping you."

"Your mother told me you didn't want me there."

"What?" Cole reeled. How could—?

Dad squinted up at him. "That's not how you felt?"

Cole's cheek twitched, giving away too much.

"Every time I drove Eddie into Seattle to spend the weekend with your mom, I asked to see you. She said you didn't want to see me."

Cole shrugged. That much was true. After the first couple of requests, he'd made a point of not being around when his dad showed up with Eddie.

"I figured I deserved the cold shoulder and it would be wrong to pressure you to change your mind, so I stayed away. But if I'd known you would see me, I would've been there in a heartbeat."

Cole squirmed at this complete one-eighty to what he'd thought his father felt. "In a heartbeat, if you didn't have a date. Right?" He hated the bitterness in his voice. *Holding on to your anger isn't helping Eddie.* Sherri's words whispered through his mind. And, yes, in his head he knew God wanted him to forgive his dad, but somehow that felt like condoning what he'd done.

Dad returned his attention to the clipboard, not rising to Cole's goading.

"He's in here." A nurse ushered a young woman pushing an elderly woman in a wheelchair into the waiting area and then turned to Dad. "This woman was telling me about your good deed this evening and I told her that you were here. I thought you'd like to hear how well she's doing."

He smiled at the woman, hunched sideways in the wheelchair, her arms curled against her chest. "How are you feeling?"

The woman nodded and smiled. "Better."

The young woman reached over the patient's head, offering her hand. "I'm Lucille. Her daughter. Thank you so much for helping Mom find her nitroglycerin and staying with her until the ambulance came."

Cole's eyes widened. He hadn't been hitting on someone?

"It was no trouble at all," Dad said magnanimously, but Cole didn't miss the hitch in his voice. No doubt thinking about Eddie.

The women left, and Cole reamed out Dad. "Why didn't you set me straight when I accused you of flirting with some woman while Eddie was waiting for you?"

"Would you have believed me?"

Cole flinched. *No. Probably not.* Sherri's voice whispered through his mind once more. *You need to forgive him.* He blew out a heavy sigh. "I'm sorry. I've been so angry with you for the way you treated Mom that I haven't treated you any better." He pressed his clenched fists to the sides of his leg, forced his fingers to straighten. Inhaled. "Can you forgive me?"

Tears sprang to Dad's eyes as he pulled Cole into a bear hug. "I'm sorry I hurt you. I've missed you so much."

Cole soaked in the love pouring from his dad like a parched desert soaked in water. "I've missed you, too." Except as he stood there wrapped in his father's arms, his thoughts returned to Eddie. If his brother hadn't run away in a snit because of their dad, then he really had taken those pills because of him. Cole stepped back. *You win.* Was Eddie that jealous of the attention he'd shown Sherri?

Jealous enough to be behind the attacks against her?

Cole paced the room, trying to wrap his head around that thought. What if Ted had been telling the truth? Eddie had been in more than a few of the photos Ted had snapped of Sherri over the past few months. And they only had Eddie's word that another guy had goaded him into raiding her ambulance and going to the drug house. He could've paid off a friend to make the phone calls, to pull that stunt in the mall and then blame it on Ted when they were caught, to sic the Rottweiler on Sherri.

Cole shook his head. Where would Eddie find

a guy with a Rottweiler who could home in on Sherri on command and ignore everyone else?

The nurse returned and ushered them into Eddie's room.

He was still unconscious, but from Cole's experience in Seattle, waiting to question addicts who'd been given Narcan, it meant Eddie would soon be alert. He'd wake up swinging but be lucid enough to answer questions.

The doctor at his bedside hooked his stethoscope around his neck and turned to them. "You're welcome to stay with him. He's stable, but we don't know when or if he'll regain consciousness."

"If?" Dad's voice cracked.

"I'm sorry to be so blunt," the doctor continued. "His vitals are good, but we don't know how long he was in cardiac arrest before the paramedic revived him. I'm afraid he could have suffered significant brain damage."

Cole closed his eyes, a lump balling in his throat.

"I've ordered an MRI, which will give us a better picture of where he's at," the doctor added then left with the nurse.

Dad sank into a chair beside Eddie's bed and clasped his hand. "We don't want to lose you, son. We need you. You hear me?"

Cole took up a chair on the other side of the

bed and echoed his father's sentiments. "I should call Mom. She'll want to be here."

Dad brought Eddie's hand to his lips. "I already did. She's on her way."

Someone shook Cole's shoulder, and his head bobbed up from his chest, his stiff muscles screaming in protest as he jerked to a sitting position. "Is Eddie awake?"

A different nurse than the one who'd taken care of his brother last night smiled down at him. "Yes, and your father wants you to hurry."

It had still been dark when Cole had retreated to the visiting area, but now bright sunlight filtered past the window blinds. Apparently he'd done more than just drift off for a few minutes.

Dad intercepted him outside Eddie's room. "He says he didn't take any pills. That he was drugged. And he's babbling about some picture you showed him."

Cole's heart rioted. He rushed past his dad, replaying last night's scene through his mind. But nothing gelled. He'd been so focused on Eddie, thinking he'd tried to kill himself, desperately afraid he'd succeeded, that all he could remember of the scene was Sherri's clearheaded determination not to give up on trying to save him. He should have called her last night, updated her on how Eddie was doing.

Dark circles ringed Eddie's sunken eyes, but they shone with a glint of determination as he strained to push up onto his elbows. "It was the guy in the picture you showed me, Cole."

Cole rested a hand on Eddie's rail-thin arm, urging him to still, wishing he could do the same to the urgency clambering up his chest. He needed information. Reliable information. Because if Eddie was telling the truth about not taking those pills—Cole's heart missed a beat—someone had tried to kill him. "Tell me everything you remember."

Eddie's eyes darted every which way as he strung together odd bits of memory.

Trying to make sense of them, Cole had to wonder how much of Eddie's story was in his imagination.

"Where did you go when you left the video store?" Dad prodded.

Eddie's eyes suddenly aligned, and he nodded vigorously. "Yes, the video store. He came in when I was checking out action movies. And he said *doing* weird."

Cole met Dad's eyes over Eddie's sweating, jerky movements. But his frown-shrug said he couldn't make sense out of what Eddie was saying, either.

"Doing weird?" Cole repeated.

"Yeah, he doesn't say it like us. Not dew-ing. He says doy-ing."

"O-kay."

Eddie pulled at his hair, looking equally frustrated that they weren't following his logic. "That's how the guy who tipped me off about Sherri's ambulance talked. I've never heard anyone else say *doing* that way."

Cole's pulse skyrocketed. "The bald guy did this to you?"

Eddie shook his head. "He wasn't bald."

"But you said—"

"I know, but this guy had hair and was better built. Except I couldn't shake the way he said *doing* out of my head. I spied on him around the end of the video rack and when he turned to leave, I saw his face. He was the guy in the picture you showed me."

"Which guy? I showed you a lot of pictures."

"The guy." Eddie tugged at his hair as if trying to pull more information from his brain. "The guy."

Cole whipped out his phone to pull up the pictures he had on it of Sherri's former partner and of Zeke's nephew.

"I followed him out," Eddie went on, "to see where he'd go. He veered behind the store and when I rounded the corner, he zapped me."

"Zapped you?" Cole stopped thumbing through the photos and met Eddie's gaze. "He had a stun gun?"

"I guess." Eddie stroked the back of his neck and turning, showed them the mark it left. "Next thing I knew, he was propping me up in a car and pouring whiskey down my throat." Tears leaked from the corners of Eddie's eyes. "I tried to stop him, but I couldn't make my arms work right. Then he untied a rubber tube from my arm and said I did good and left."

Dad grabbed Eddie's arm, exposing a nasty bruise on the inside of his elbow. "He shot him up."

Cole quickly thumbed through the rest of his pictures. If this guy had just been worried about Eddie identifying him, he'd have drugged him in some back alley to make it look like he OD'd. This was meant to be more—another dig at him. Cole showed Eddie the photo he'd snapped of Zeke's nephew. "Is this the guy?"

Eddie blinked away tears, trembling viciously. "No, not him. The other guy."

Cole sprang to his feet, his mind veering to the look on Sherri's face when the deputy had handed him the suicide note. She'd been the target, not him. He flipped back to the photo he'd snapped of Joe in the coffee shop. "Him?"

"Yeah, him."

Forcing calm into his voice, Cole gave Eddie's shoulder a squeeze. "You did good. I'll call and have a deputy pick him up. Be right back." Cole stepped into the hall, cell phone to his ear, his heart galloping ahead to the next call he needed to make. To Sherri.

Zeke, in uniform, strode toward him. "How's your brother? I just heard."

Cole swallowed his surprise that Zeke would make a special trip to the hospital to check on him. Sure they were partners, but it wasn't as if Zeke liked him. "He's going to be okay." Cole filled him in on the assault and the arrest warrant he'd been about to request for Joe Martello.

Zeke squeezed Cole's shoulder supportively. "I'll pick him up myself. It's still crazy at the station, handling calls on the missing infant. I'm glad your brother's okay." Zeke must've sensed Cole's stunned reaction to his sudden show of support. "I might not have wanted you to get this job, but I lost my sister to drugs," he explained. "I wouldn't wish it on anyone."

"I'm sorry. I didn't know."

Zeke flinched. "Some pothead lured her to Seattle, got her hooked on harder stuff, so she resorted to turning tricks to pay for her habit. By the time I tracked her down..."

His voice trailed off, and Cole's mind flipped

back to Zeke's seething anger when they'd caught up to the kids outside the schoolyard. Cole swiped his hand over his face, ashamed by how seriously he'd misjudged the man.

Zeke shook off the dark mask that had fallen over his face. "I'll go pick this guy up before he can do any more damage."

"I appreciate it." Cole dialed Sherri's cell phone to update her on the situation and to warn her to stay at her parents' until they had Joe in custody. Her phone went straight to voice mail, and an uneasy feeling rippled through his stomach. She'd intended to drive her car back to her parents', but would she have driven it after finding Eddie inside?

He disconnected without leaving a message and called her folks' number. "Mrs. Steele, this is Cole Donovan. Is—"

"Oh, how's your brother?"

"Good." Her voice sounded sleepy, and he glanced at his watch. Five in the morning. He probably should've waited to call.

"We haven't stopped praying since Sherri told us what happened."

Cole relaxed at the news that she was there. "Thank you. I appreciate that. He should recover fine, thanks to Sherri. She was amazing last night. She refused to give up on him."

"Yes, that's our Sherri."

Cole could hear the smile in her voice. "Is she up yet? May I speak to her?"

"Isn't she with you?"

His heart lightened. "No. How long ago did she leave?"

"Leave?" Concern rippled through Mrs. Steele's voice. "She never came home last night. She called and told us what happened. I assumed..."

"It's okay. She must be at her apartment. I didn't think to try there. I rode to the hospital on the ambulance and assumed she'd head back to your place after the deputies finished with her car." But of course, she wouldn't have wanted to drive it. Probably wouldn't have wanted to face a night in her parents' house after almost losing Eddie. He hated to imagine the nightmares that must've haunted her last night. He'd been so consumed with guilt. He hadn't thought about how finding Eddie like that had to be eating away at her.

He scrolled through his contact list, highlighted her apartment's home phone number and hit Connect. After five rings, it went to voicemail. "Hey, Sherri. It's Cole. Call me as soon as you get this message. It's important." *Please, Lord, let her just be screening her calls.* But even as the prayer whispered past his lips, a chill shivered down his spine. If Joe had a key to Sherri's car, he could have a key to her apartment, too. Cole hurried back to his brother's room. "Do you remember how Joe got into Sherri's car? Did he have a key?"

Eddie shook his head. "I don't know. I didn't come to until he'd already shoved me inside."

"Is Sherri okay?" The concern in Dad's voice stirred up the acid already burning Cole's gut.

"I don't know. I couldn't—" Her keys were found on the mall floor. Joe must've *borrowed* them to make an imprint. *Or Zeke's nephew had.* Cole shot a look toward the hall, suddenly doubting Zeke's kid-sister story. "I couldn't get a hold of her."

"Then you need to go find her."

Everything in him was already halfway out the door, but— Cole looked to Eddie.

"Go!"

He raced out to the parking lot and searched the lot for where the deputy had parked his truck. He punched the button on his fob and ran toward the sound of the horn. Swinging into the driver's seat, he tried Sherri's cell phone number again, slid the phone into its holder and swerved out of the lot.

On the third ring, the phone clicked on.

"Sherri? Sherri, are you there?"

"Cole, is that you? I'm sorry the reception's terrible here."

"Where are you?"

"What's wrong? Is Eddie—?"

He mentally kicked himself for causing her more panic. "He's awake. He's going to be okay." Cole explained how Joe drugged him, and assured her that Eddie wasn't jealous of her. "We've issued an arrest warrant. But he's still at large. Where are you?"

"I'm running on the trail along the river."

Cole cranked a U-turn at the next intersection and sped toward the trailhead. "Get back to the parking lot now. I'm coming to get you. I'll be there in seven minutes."

"You don't have to do that. I'll be fine. I'll go back to my parents'. Your brother needs you."

"You may be fine, but I won't be until I know you're safe and that psycho ex-partner of yours is behind bars." The phone crackled. "Sherri? Did you hear me? Get back to the trailhead now. And be careful."

"Cole? I hear a baby crying?" The phone garbled.

"Sherri. *Sherri!*"

"I'm just going to—" The phone cut out.

Cole floored the gas pedal.

FIFTEEN

Sherri cocked her ear toward the path ahead, every muscle primed to rush into action. The sound of the river's rushing water. Songbirds welcoming the day. *There it was again.* Definitely a baby's cry. She jogged ahead a few paces and the sound shifted. Coming from the riverbank. She peered down at the tangled vegetation hiding the river's edge from view. "Hello, is someone there? Do you need help?"

An image of baby Moses, floating downriver in a little boat sprang to mind, only this river was no gentle stream and with the snow still melting off the mountain peaks, it was frigid. If the child's parent had fallen in… The cries grew louder. More desperate.

She scrambled down the riverbank, slipping and sliding on the precarious slope. "It's okay, baby, I'm coming." She clawed through the brambles at the bottom, landing her first step out the other side right into icy water. She jerked back, clinging to the prickly bushes to keep from teetering off the edge.

The cries rose up to her right. Very close.

"Shh, now, it's okay." Sherri dropped to her knees and crawled toward the inconsolable whimpers. She swept aside rotted leaves and twigs, exposing a small animal's den cut into the bank. Her stomach flip-flopped. Had it been a baby fox or other wild animal she'd heard?

The cries sounded again.

Very human.

What kind of monster would leave a child in a fox's den? She clawed at the dirt to reach the poor dear. "It's okay. It's okay. I've got you." She stretched her arm inside. Her fingers grazed fabric. She stretched farther, caught the edge of the fabric between her fingertips. The baby kicked, tugging the fabric from her clasp. She tunneled the opening wider and tried again.

A twig snapped behind her.

"Shush, shush, shush," she cooed to the infant, her fingers closing around a tiny foot.

Something smashed into the back of her knee.

"Ouch!" Releasing her grip, she jerked her arm out of the hole and rolled to her back. She shrank from the stranger looming over her, her hands grappling for a stick, a rock, something. "Who are you? What do you want?"

The man thumbed up the brim of his cowboy

hat, his unnaturally blue eyes laughing at her, his mouth curving into a smile as broad as his hat. "Don't you recognize me, darlin'?" The question oozed from his lips in a sickeningly sweet drawl.

She squinted at him. There was something familiar about his voice, but she couldn't place—

Her heart jolted. Bald, blue eyes, goatee, paunch belly. "You're...you're Eddie's friend."

He threw his head back and laughed. "I wouldn't call us friends."

She flipped onto her belly to push to her feet.

He yanked her hair and snapped back her head, silencing her scream with a slash of duct tape. "Just like I wouldn't call you and I *friends*."

He'd dropped the drawl, and her veins iced at the familiar voice. *Joe.* She reared to her knees to ease the pain screaming through her scalp and hoofed back a foot.

He deflected it with his shin.

Screaming uselessly, she lifted a hand to rip the tape from her mouth.

He yanked her head back farther, and something cold dug into her neck. "I wouldn't do that if I were you."

She didn't listen to him and as she yanked on the tape, electricity jolted through her body.

She fell to her back, and Joe's meaty hand, sheathed in a latex glove, silenced her cry of agony. Her muscles spasmed uncontrollably.

Grinning wickedly, he twisted the stun gun in front of her face and then pushed it back into her neck. "You going to be a good girl or do we need another lesson?"

She recoiled from the pressure.

He chuckled. "I thought you'd see it my way. It's a shame, though. I do enjoy hearing you scream." He bared his teeth in a sick leer.

"I'm sorry I cost you your job, Joe. Really I am."

"Yeah, just like my wife'll be sorry. You women are so predictable. I watched you go for a run last night after your boyfriend left," he rambled. "You'd think someone was chasing you from the way you flew."

Her skin crawled at the thought of him watching her. Stalking her. Cole had warned her not to run alone, but after finding Eddie in her car, she hadn't been able to shut the images out of her brain.

Joe's hot breath whispered over her ears. "Your inner demons chasing you? You can't escape them, you know." His voice lifted to a sympathetic falsetto. "Letting Luke die. Driving Eddie to suicide. Those'll haunt you until the day you die." He grabbed her upper arm and yanked her to her feet. "So really…I'm doing you a favor." He shoved her toward the river.

He was going to kill her. *Drown her.*

Her mind scrambled for a plan. Cole had said it would take him seven minutes to get to the parking lot. Maybe another five to reach her here…if he headed the right direction on the path and didn't race right past. If she could stall Joe, keep him talking so Cole would hear them. Joe couldn't have heard her phone call. If he'd known Cole was on his way, he wouldn't have risked showing himself here.

She started to ask about the baby, but then thought better of it. If he was focused on her, he wouldn't be hurting the baby and Cole would find the infant in time if…he was still crying.

The baby wailed, and Joe flashed a caustic glance toward the foxhole. "Shut up, kid. Be happy I saved you from that no good whore of a mother."

Sherri gasped. He'd kidnapped the baby? From his ex-wife? "You set up the attack in the mall?" Sherri blurted to distract him from the infant's cry.

"You sound surprised." He slanted her an oily smile. "But you had to suspect. The police came to see me, after all. Seemed to think I might still be sore at you. Sore enough to hurt you."

"I didn't send them. I swear. I didn't think—" Her voice broke. How'd he know how to scuttle the security? Let alone convince all those teens to risk their necks?

"You didn't think I'd still hate you?" he asked snidely. They broke through the bushes to the river's edge and, wrenching her arm behind her back, he pressed her to her knees.

She resisted the impulse to fight him, knowing another zap of the stun gun would end any chance of stalling him long enough for Cole to get to her. "I thought...I thought you were happy now."

"You of all people should know appearances are deceptive."

"Me? Why?" She strained to listen over the sound of rushing water. Was that a car door? She needed to stall him. "I...I don't know what you mean."

He chuckled. "Acting like nothing bothers you. Acting like everything that's happened to you doesn't scare you to death. Kind of hypocritical, don't you think? Telling me I need help but refusing it yourself."

"Is that what this is about? You wanted to see me break?"

He cackled. "No. My ex-wife I wanted to break. You—" he shoved her face under the water "—I wanted to *kill*."

She clawed at his hand with her only free hand, flailed her head wildly to try and escape his grip. Her lungs burned. And just when she thought she'd black out, he yanked her out. She gasped, inhaled the air in hungry gulps.

He trailed his finger along her jaw and tipped up her chin. "But tormenting you proved to be way more fun than I'd ever imagined." His maniacal gaze held hers in a chilling grip.

She swallowed hard. Somehow she needed to keep him talking. "The dispatcher. How'd you get her to help you?"

He threw his head back and laughed. "Your boyfriend figured that much out, did he? But not that she's an addict?"

"You supplied her with drugs?"

He clucked victoriously. "An addict'll do anything for a fix. And seeing your face when Atkins ranted at you at Luke's funeral was priceless."

She slipped her hand into the water. "You're sick."

"It's called justice, honey. Only right you should experience firsthand what it feels like to have someone screw around with your life." He wrenched her arm higher behind her back. "This is what you get for turning me down for that date. If you hadn't, I would've put you out of your misery that night." He shoved her face back into the water. "Instead, you gave me plenty of time to think of better ways to make you pay."

Fighting not to panic, she grappled for a rock she could pull free from the riverbed. But they were big. They were all too big. Black dots bounced in front of her eyes as the oxygen seeped from her lungs. She lurched forward and her fingers closed around a football-sized rock. Blackness crept along the edges of her vision. She levered the rock over her shoulder.

His grip broke. He fell back, clutching his head and cursing.

She scrambled downriver. But the baby's cry stopped her. She couldn't leave him alone with the baby.

"Sherri!" Cole's faint shout filtered through trees. "Where are you?"

She clambered up the riverbank. "Cole! Over here!"

Joe grabbed her foot, and she went down hard. He shoved something into her side and excruciating pain jolted through her body. "Nice try," he sneered, as a whimpered "please" dribbled from her lips and everything went black.

Sherri startled to consciousness at the bite of icy water seeping through her shoes.

"Your boyfriend's spoiling my fun," Joe hissed into her ear, his arm hooked under her armpits and around her chest as he dragged her across a shallow part of the river. He paused in the center and planted her on her feet.

A roar filled her ears. She swayed, straining to gain her bearings.

He clutched the back of her head and forced her gaze to the ground.

Her heart dropped. They stood on the precipice of a ten-foot waterfall.

"But I'm thinking he'll dive in after you." He cackled. "Make for some good target practice."

Sherri jerked back her head, felt the moment it connected with his nose.

The next instant his shove sent her freefalling.

SIXTEEN

A crash of water swallowed Sherri's scream and ripped through Cole's heart. He barreled down the riverbank, plowing blindly through the vegetation. At a break in the bushes, he caught sight of a bald guy at the top of the falls, feet braced apart, a gun aimed at the river below. Joe? Skidding to a stop, Cole drew his off-duty pistol from his ankle holster and squeezed off a shot. The bullet pinged the rocks and sent the man racing for cover.

Sherri's cry rose from the water and was immediately swallowed again.

Cole dashed to the river's edge. "Hang on! I'm coming." He glanced up the other side of the bank, and seeing no sign of Joe taking a bead on them, tucked his gun in the back of his jeans and dove in.

The icy temperature stole his breath as the wicked undercurrent grabbed at his legs. *Sherri, hang on*, he willed, straining to see her through the inky blackness. His lungs burning, he clawed his way to the surface and whirled in circles, searching. The churning eddies made it impossible to see. "Sherri!" *Oh, God, show me where she is.*

Gunfire cracked the air, pebbled the water.

Blood swirled to the surface.

"No!" Cole dove under, flailing wildly, his heart screaming. His fingers grazed something. Clothing. He dug in with an iron grip and roared upward. The instant they broke the surface, he hauled her against his chest, swept the hair from her face. "I got you."

She sputtered, and his heart kicked back into rhythm.

Clutching her with one arm, he surged toward shore. The powerful undertow tugged back, refusing to release her. She started to slip from his grip and cried out, grasped his shirt.

He curled his arm more tightly around her, kicked harder. "I'm not letting go!"

A gunshot hissed past his ear. It came from shore, too near where he was headed. Another shot slapped the water beside him. He shifted his body to shield Sherri, as his foot hit rock, found purchase on the riverbed. "We're almost there!"

She got her feet under her and fire seemed to surge through her veins. "The baby. He's going for the baby."

Baby? Was Joe the kidnapper? They tried to run for shore. But it was like wading in waist-deep molasses.

Another shot rang out, and Sherri's body ricocheted against his chest. She went limp and slipped under the water in a swirl of red.

"No!" Cole heaved her out of the water and rocketed for shore.

Edging under the cover of bushes, he clasped the back of her neck and eased her to the ground. His stomach lurched at the red circle blooming over her chest. He whipped off his shirt and pressed it to the bullet wound. His heart scrunched up into his ribs. Her pallor was pasty white, her lips purple, the rise and fall of her chest barely perceptible. "Stay with me, Sherri. You're going to be okay."

Sirens grew louder. Finally, the backup he'd called for.

The sound of Joe lashing through the bushes rose a few hundred feet to his left. And getting closer, despite the deputies closing in.

Cole dragged Sherri deeper under cover and with one hand continuing pressure on her wound, he reached for the gun he'd jammed in the back of his pants. His fist clenched. The gun was gone. Now what?

A pitiful cry filtered through the trees.

Sherri's eyes sprang open—wild and panicked.

"The baby. You have to save the baby." The order came out scarcely louder than a whisper.

"Shh," Cole whispered. "It's okay. Help is on the way." He stroked wet strands of hair from her face, willing into his gaze a reassurance that with her warm blood seeping through the drenched cloth and over his fingers, he didn't feel.

The baby wailed again, and Sherri wrestled against his hand holding her down, lashing her head from side to side.

Cole cupped his free hand around her head, straining to keep her still. "Easy," he whispered, his lips grazing hers. "I'm here. And I'm not leaving you."

Sherri's heart ached at the promise she'd been longing to hear for too many years. "I love you, Cole. I've always loved you."

His hot tears splashed onto her cheeks. "Stay with me, Sherri."

Her chest was on fire, but she felt cold. So cold. And it hurt to breathe. Scrounging up all her strength, she lifted her hand to cover his. "I'm fine. You need to save the baby." Her heart lurched at the words—Luke's words, his plea to her. A bewildering peace cradled her as darkness edged her vision. With astounding clarity she realized that this was what Luke had felt, what he'd wanted her to know.

"The paramedics will take care of him," Cole assured and then yelled up the bank, "Down here. We have a gunshot wound to the chest. Hurry!"

A gunshot sliced through the leaves, and Cole hunched over her, shielding her.

The baby's cry punctuated the sounds of splashing water.

Cole squinted through the trees toward the river. "The idiot's trying to cross the river with the baby. Down here! He's getting away," he shouted, but the responding voices sounded far too far away.

"Cole." She gasped, struggling to suck in enough air to push out the words. "I'm okay. I want you to save the baby."

"You're not okay," he shouted, his expression tortured. "I won't leave you."

The sound of splashing water stopped, then a sickening plop swallowed the baby's cry.

Her heart rioted. Tears burned her eyes. "Please, Cole. Save him for me."

He pressed a desperate kiss to her lips and then bolted to his feet. At the sound of Cole hitting the water, her eyes slipped closed.

Searing pain ignited in her chest as a baby's cry tugged her from sweet oblivion.

"Decreased lung sounds on the right," a male

voice grumbled. "Possible pneumo. She's having a hard time breathing."

The ground beneath her rumbled and bounced. Her mind flailed from sensation to sound, struggling to make sense of them. Inhaling, she startled at the odd pressure. She strained to open her eyes, caught glimpses of faces, the inside of an ambulance, before her eyelids fluttered, closed of their own volition. "Cole?"

A warm hand curled around hers. "I'm right here. Along with the little guy whose life you saved." He propped up the bundle cradled in his blanket-clad arms for her to see.

The baby! "He's okay?"

"Yes, and Joe is in custody."

"Sorry, I doubted you about Joe," Dan said from her other side. He flicked his finger against a lethal-looking needle.

She tugged the oxygen mask from her mouth. "What are you doing with that?"

He fitted the mask back in place with a stern, don't-touch look. "Demerol for the pain."

She relaxed back against the gurney. "Thank you."

Dan gave her the needle, then relieved Cole of the baby.

Bending over her, Cole tenderly stroked her hair. "You are one incredible woman."

"That's our superwoman," Dan cooed to the

baby. "This is the second time she's saved your life. Do you know that?"

Cole smoothed her furrowed brow and shook his head. "I don't think math was your partner's best subject." He winked and turned to Dan. "How do you figure twice?"

Dan stepped up to the end of the gurney and showed her the baby. "This is Luke Gibson."

Tears clogged Sherri's throat.

Cole's hand tightened around hers, his gaze searching her face. "What's wrong? Are you in pain?"

She pulled the mask from her mouth. "Mary Gibson is the woman whose husband assaulted her and then shot my partner."

"Sherri saved her and the baby," Dan filled in, pride beaming from his eyes. "And the mother had promised to name the child after Luke if it was a boy, or Sherri if it was a girl." Dan squeezed her toe. "Luke would've been proud of you."

The tears spilled to her cheeks.

Cole pressed a kiss to her damp cheek and whispered close to her ear, "You did good."

She shook her head. "It's because of me Joe kidnapped the poor thing in the first place. He must've known the connection and known how it would torment me."

The paramedic driving said, "More likely he took the kid to torment his ex-wife. He was livid when he first heard she was pregnant after she left him."

Cole's attention swerved to the front of the ambulance. "Wait, you're saying this baby's mother is Joe's ex-wife?"

"Yeah, you didn't know?"

"No." Cole looked at her.

"I didn't know. Joe and his wife had split before I was hired. I'd never met her." Her mind whirled, her breaths coming fast and shallow.

Dan fit her oxygen mask back in place. "I didn't know, either. I knew his ex-wife's name was Mary, but of course her last name's different now. I never made the connection."

Sherri tugged the mask away. "Joe told me he wanted to break his wife. I thought—"

This time Cole commandeered the mask from her grasp and held it in place. "It's okay. We've caught him red-handed on kidnapping and attempted murder. He won't be able to hurt her or you anymore."

But…but…Joe's rant replayed through her mind. Something he'd said didn't line up. She could sense it, but couldn't sort out what it was.

The ambulance swerved into the hospital's driveway and within seconds her gurney was being yanked from the back of the truck. Cole strode beside her. "I'll be right here when you get out of surgery." He smiled down at her. "We have a lot to talk about."

The gurney surged through the doors, and he slid from her view. She grappled for his hand. "Wait!"

Cole leaned over her with a warmth in his eyes that stole her breath. He stroked her hair and then cradled her cheek in his palm. "You need to let the doctors do their job."

"It's about Joe." She pulled the mask from her face. "He said, 'My wife, I wanted to break. You I wanted to kill.'"

Cole's expression turned all gooey tender, his face hovering closer. "You're safe now."

She closed her eyes and scrunched her forehead, straining for a way to make him understand when she wasn't sure it made sense herself. "He said he *wanted*—past tense—to kill me, but after Luke's death, decided tormenting me was more fun."

Cole nodded, but he didn't seem to understand at all.

"Don't you see? I was supposed to die. Not Luke."

The nurses whisked Sherri away before Cole could respond to her anguished cry. His heart ached to see how much the man's death still tormented her. After today her nightmares were bound to get worse than ever.

Zeke must've come to the hospital to get her statement, because he stepped up beside Cole and squeezed his shoulder. "She might be onto something."

"What are you talking about?" The air conditioning chilled the water dripping from his clothes. Shivering, he tugged closed the blanket Dan had given him to warm up after his plunge in the river. "You think Joe had something to do with Luke's death?"

"Could be we arrested the wrong guy for his murder."

"How? The man assaulted his wife to the point of almost losing her baby then shot at the paramedics who came to save them. How do you get that wrong?" Cole didn't like the look of the twitch in Zeke's cheek.

"Mary's testimony was sketchy. She came home from her morning exercise class and the door was unlocked. She heard what she assumed was her new husband upstairs. When she went up, he shoved her downstairs and repeatedly kicked her in the gut. Her description of the man—shorts and running shirt, dark hair—fit her husband's, but later she claimed she never actually saw him and knew he'd never hurt her. He wanted this baby as much as she did, or so she said." Zeke shrugged. "We figured she was a typical abused woman, defending her abuser."

"You must have had other evidence."

"Yeah, a 9-1-1 call from the house, claiming to be from her husband. Voice recognition software was inconclusive on a match."

"But it doesn't make sense that a burglar caught by the homeowner would waste time calling 9-1-1 after beating her up."

"Exactly. And the husband came in from his usual—" Zeke air-quoted the word "—morning run just after the ambulance pulled away with his wife inside. He played the part of the frantic husband real well. But the shot that took out Luke came from a rifle we recovered from the woods behind the house. His rifle. And the only witnesses that saw him running, saw him running from the direction of those woods."

"Gunfire residue?"

"No, but he was wearing a sleeveless shirt and had already been to the washroom before we thought to check."

"Where's this guy now?"

"In jail awaiting trial. Refused a plea bargain. Says he's innocent."

Cole sighed, not knowing what to think. "If the assailant was her ex-husband, surely she would've recognized him."

Dan joined them, his arms loaded with the

supplies needed to restock his rig. "You talking about Joe?"

"Yeah."

"His wife walked out on him three years ago. At the time, he was fifty pounds heavier, had a full beard and scraggly hair. None of us recognized him when he first got out of rehab."

"You think his wife wouldn't have recognized him?"

Dan shrugged. "She'd just been shoved down the stairs. She wouldn't be noticing much of anything. It took me a few minutes to recognize him today in that disguise he had on, and I was staring at him. And he was always good at mimicking voices."

"Why didn't you tell us this eight months ago when Luke was shot?" Zeke seethed.

"Whoa." Dan backed up a step. "I had no reason to think you'd arrested the wrong man."

"Okay, looks like we'll have a lot more questions for Joe Martello." Zeke clapped Cole on the shoulder. "Don't worry. We'll nail this guy for everything we can get on him. You're a good man. I'm sorry I was tough on you."

Cole shook his hand. "Apology accepted. I think we were all guilty of misjudging each other."

"Yeah, you want a lift back to the trailhead to pick up your truck?"

"Not right now, thanks. I need to stay here. I have to check on Eddie. And I promised Sherri I wasn't leaving." It had ripped his heart out to abandon her on the riverbank and go after the baby. He wasn't about to get any farther from her than the doctors made him.

He found a quiet corner and let his eyes slip closed. *Please, Lord, let her be okay.* Her tortured cry as the nurse had wheeled her away, that she was supposed to die not Luke, replayed in his mind, squeezed his chest. He couldn't pretend for another second that his heart didn't belong to her. Had always been hers. But would she ever get past the nightmares and self-torment enough to let him in?

SEVENTEEN

Cole couldn't remember a more perfect afternoon. The sun was shining. The birds were singing. And every last one of Sherri's extended family had gathered at her uncle's farm to celebrate her recovery.

The first bullet that'd caught her had grazed her arm, causing no serious damage. The second bullet had hit just under her left collarbone and thankfully hadn't punctured a lung. But between the exertion and holding her breath in the cold water, she'd developed spontaneous pneumothorax. Needless to say, he'd spent a lot of time on his knees praying in the ten long days since. Now they sat shoulder to shoulder at a long line of picnic tables overflowing with everything from quinoa salad to fried chicken and home-baked buns, and Sherri was absolutely glowing.

Unlike the past few months, she talked freely about all the bad things that had been happening to her and why she'd been so reluctant to admit they were overwhelming her. "Cole helped me see that I wasn't helping anyone, including myself, by pretending nothing was wrong." She choked up.

He reached for her hand beneath the table and offered an encouraging smile.

Squeezing his fingers like a lifeline, she returned her attention to her family. "So I'm making it my mission to help others not make the same mistakes I did."

Pride swelled Cole's chest. She'd already met with her colleagues and admitted to the PTSD symptoms she'd battled following her partner's murder, and one by one they'd each admitted to their own personal struggles, some openly, some confiding in her afterward through calls and notes and thanking her for her transparency.

Sherri's aunt passed him a plate of cookies, snapping him out of his musing. "What ever happened to that young man who tried to save Sherri from those hooligans in the mall?"

Shame pinged Cole's heart for doubting Ted's motives for rushing to protect Sherri. "He's recovered from the assault and is doing well." And thankfully had promised to curb his obsessive concern for her welfare.

"And what about your brother? How's he doing?"

"Better. Thank you for asking." Eddie had

changed a lot since his brush with death. He was getting counseling and they were all working at communicating better. "We're hopeful he'll overcome his destructive behavior without the need for a residential rehab."

"I'm so glad. You should bring him with you to next Sunday's picnic. We'd love to have him."

"That's very kind of you," Cole replied, choking down his surprise. He still couldn't quite believe Sherri's family hadn't balked at their growing closeness considering her father's initial reception the day of the dog attack. A guy with a family as broken as Cole's was a long way from what most parents would want for their only daughter. But a few hours in her family's company had more than convinced him that he'd been an idiot to think he'd be happier single.

He fingered the small box in his pocket, his heart somersaulting.

After the meal, the kids ran off to play and the adults retired to lawn chairs under the trees. He'd hoped to coax Sherri into a romantic walk through the meadow, but so many of her cousins were eager to talk with her that he ended up relinquishing his place at her side and joining the men.

Jake plunked down beside him and handed him a glass of lemonade. "You're good for her, you know. I haven't seen her this happy in a long time."

"I'm glad she's happy." Cole soaked in the sight of the light in her eyes, the tiny creases at their edges that were thanks to her beaming smile, her rosy cheeks, the way the breeze teased her hair, blowing it over her lips so she had to keep brushing it away.

"Oh, man—" Jake laughed at him "—you've got it bad."

Oh, yeah. Cole reined in a private smile and sipped his lemonade.

"Do you still have nightmares, Sherri?" Jake's father, the former sheriff, asked.

Cole's heart galloped as everyone went silent. She'd once scoffed that no man would want to marry a woman who spent half the night thrashing in her sleep.

"Not nearly as bad or as frequent as before." Her gaze sought his and held. "Cole told me they would ease if I talked about them, but I think it was seeing the tortured look on his face when I begged him to save Baby Luke that made the difference. You see—" her voice hitched and Cole had to grip the arms of his lawn chair to stop himself from springing to her side and pulling her into his arms. "People could tell me all they wanted that there was nothing I could've done to save Luke, but I still felt as if I'd let him down. But when I begged Cole to save the baby, I honestly didn't think I was going to make it."

The admission slammed the air from his chest. He closed his eyes against the throbbing pain at the mere thought of losing her. And from the sound of the sniffles coming from the circle of family, he wasn't alone.

Sherri knelt beside him and clasped his hand, before he'd realized she'd crossed the lawn between them. "I could see he didn't want to leave my side. But I didn't want him to stay and watch me die when he could save another. I think God allowed me to feel what Luke had felt when he was dying. He'd wanted me to save that mother and child more than anything, just like I'd wanted Cole to save the baby." Tears spilled from her eyes. "And in that moment, I knew I hadn't let Luke down."

Cole tugged her into his arms. Cradling her against his heart, he buried his face in her hair. "Please don't ever ask me to leave you again."

She lifted her head and palmed his tear-dampened shirt with a shy smile. "I won't."

His heart swelled to bursting and forgetting about her family he lowered his head and claimed her lips with a sweet, lingering kiss.

As a chorus of "ahs" rose around them, her lips curved into a smile beneath his. Her arms slipped around his neck, and she whispered close to his ear. "Now my family knows all my secrets."

The family kindly turned the spotlight off

them, delving into conversations about the weather and the gardens with only a few giggles and whispers from her younger cousins. Sherri's cheeks had turned a gorgeous shade of pink, but she didn't seem in any hurry to leave his arms. If he'd needed any more assurance that she wasn't ashamed of him, or his family, that confirmed it.

Jake caught his attention, and wrapping his arm around his own wife, winked.

Sherri nibbled on her bottom lip as Cole walked her to her apartment, his hands stuffed in his pockets. He'd grown fidgety after their kiss at the picnic, asking when the gathering usually broke up and if she wanted to leave early, but...not in a twinkly eyed I-can't-wait-to-get-you-alone-to-kiss-you-again kind of way. Fishing her key from her purse, she slanted a glance his direction. "Are you okay?"

His head snapped up, surprise on his face. "Never better." He pulled his hands from his pockets and wrapped an arm around her waist. "Your family is terrific. Thanks for inviting me."

She chuckled. "Mom has been talking about you so much. My aunts would've come looking for you themselves if I hadn't."

The twinkle she'd been missing returned to his eyes.

Sherri unlocked her apartment door and waved

him inside, but instead of whirling her into his arms, he sauntered over to the dining table.

"You finished the teddy bear puzzle."

Her heart skipped at the pleased note to his voice.

She joined him at the table and smiled at the image of the teddy bear nurse bandaging the other bear's paw. Her finger strayed to the hole in the bear's chest where a couple of pieces were missing. "Some pieces were missing." She couldn't help the melancholy that seeped into her voice, remembering how disappointed she'd felt the first time she'd done the puzzle. She'd left it on the table for months, hoping the pieces would turn up…hoping he would turn up. But when months had gone by with no sign of either, it had seemed cruelly appropriate that it was the bear's heart that was missing. The one thing Cole hadn't been willing to let her mend.

Cole reached into his pocket and presented her with a tiny box.

Her breath caught at the sight of it, at his broad smile, and all she could do was stare. If it was what it looked like, shouldn't he be asking her something first?

As if he'd read her mind, he blushed and flipped open the lid. A plain brown, hand-cut, jigsaw-shaped cardboard piece sat in the bottom of the velvet-lined box. "I'd noticed the pieces were missing when I dropped in after work yesterday and when you were in the other room, I traced the shape of the gap so I could make a piece to fit."

She stared at it, speechless, amazed by how sweet that was and yet vaguely disappointed that something else hadn't been in the box.

Smiling, he set the box on the table and rubbed the puzzle piece between his fingers. "The day I gave you this puzzle I was already a little bit in love with you. I was sure you could make just about anything better."

"Except your heart," she said softly.

A smile teased his lips. "Yeah, except that." He turned the puzzle piece over and fit it into the hole in the bear's chest. "I know better now."

A teeny squeal slipped out at the sight of the heart he'd painted in bold shades of red on the other side of the puzzle piece. On the corner of the heart, he'd painted crisscrossed bandages. She leaned closer and traced her finger over the image, awed by the detail. "I can't believe you did this for me. It's…perfect. Now I can frame the puzzle and give it a place of honor over my couch."

He scooped up her hand and brought it to his lips. "I was hoping we might hang it over our couch."

Blinking, she looked from his lips pressed tc

her fingers to the earnestness in his gaze, and swallowed the bubble of happiness clogging her throat. *"Our* couch?"

"Sherri, I love you more than I ever imagined it possible to love. I meant what I said this afternoon. I don't ever want to leave you. You already have my heart. Will you—" he cocked his head to the side, suddenly looking as fidgety as he'd been earlier, and a smile bloomed inside her, now that she understood the reason "—take the rest of me? Will you marry me?"

She bounded into his arms, her mouth finding his, saying without words all that was in her heart. He held her close, responding with a lingering kiss, soft and tender and brimming with emotions she'd scarcely allowed herself to feel for a long, long while. Slowly, he pulled away, his lips curving into a smile that filled her with warmth.

His hands cradled her face, as his smoky gaze searched hers in a gentle caress. "Is that a yes? Because I'd really like to hear the words."

Laughter bubbled inside her at the hint of uncertainty in his voice, in this man who alone had seen through her pretenses and had challenged her to bare her heart. Did he truly doubt that kiss meant anything other than what it appeared to?

She covered his hands with her own. "Cole, I've admired you for as long as I can remember. But these past few weeks have shown me how truly remarkable you are. I thank God every day for bringing you back into my life. You are caring and protective and brutally perceptive." She smiled at the blush that crept into his cheeks. "And I'm so glad you refused to let me hide behind my facades. I love you with all of my heart, and nothing would make me happier than to be your wife."

With an exultant "whoop" he lifted her from the ground and twirled her in a joyous circle. He pulled her into another kiss. One she hoped would never stop.

* * * * *

Dear Reader,

This novel proved to be a surprising challenge to write, thanks to Sherri's tendency to pretend everything is okay and not ask for help. One astute reader told me she's a perfectionist, which surprised me, although after looking up the characteristics, I could see her point. Sherri definitely didn't want to fail, or to let others down, especially God.

Some people have an easier time admitting to weakness or seeking help than others. While many inadvertently resent a lack of help from loved ones or friends, without realizing that because they hadn't asked for help, their friends had no idea of their need. I deeply appreciate people who can be transparent about their struggles, especially in a desire to help others wade through similar difficulties. Many First Responders struggle to live with the horrific scenes they've witnessed, while others struggle to live with a personal loss or tragedy or illness. What I hope this story helps each of us to see is that being willing to open up about our own struggles, or inviting others to open up to us, however uncomfortable that might feel, can go a long way to mending fractured hearts.

I'd love to hear from you. You can reach me

via email at SandraOrchard@ymail.com, or at facebook.com/SandraOrchard. To learn more about all my novels and explore fun bonus features, please visit me online at www.SandraOrchard.com and sign up for my newsletter for exclusive subscriber giveaways.

Sincerely,

Sandra Orchard